THE AUSTRALIANS

BEGUILED AND BEDAZZLED

Victoria Gordon

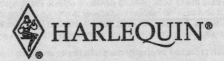

HARLEQUIN®

TORONTO • NEW YORK • LONDON
AMSTERDAM • PARIS • SYDNEY • HAMBURG
STOCKHOLM • ATHENS • TOKYO • MILAN • MADRID
PRAGUE • WARSAW • BUDAPEST • AUCKLAND

ISBN 0-373-82576-5

BEGUILED AND BEDAZZLED

First North American Publication 1998.

Welcome to Harlequin's great new series,
created by some of our bestselling authors
from Down Under:

~ THE AUSTRALIANS ~

Twelve tales of heated romance and adventure—
guaranteed to turn your whole world upside down!

Travel to an Outback cattle station, experience the
glamour of the Gold Coast or visit the bright lights
of Sydney where you'll meet twelve engaging young
women, all feisty and all about to face their biggest
challenge yet...falling in love.

And it will take some very special women to tame
our heroes! Strong, rugged, often infuriating and
always irresistible, they're one hundred percent prime
Australian male: hard to get close to...but even
harder to forget!

The Wonder from Down Under:
where spirited women win the hearts of
Australia's most independent men.

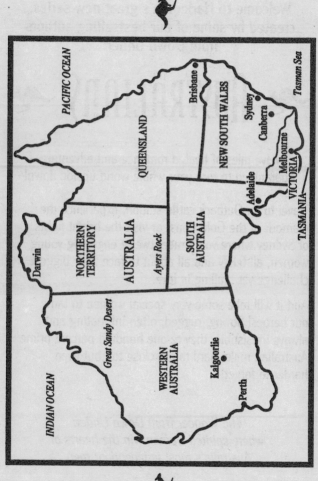

Victoria Gordon is a former journalist who began writing romances in 1979. Canadian-born, she moved to Australia in the early '70s and now lives in northern Tasmania. She has judged retrieving trials for gundogs and is active in a variety of other outdoor activities when not chained to her magic word-processing machine.

CHAPTER ONE

COLLEEN listened to the beeps, then counted the telephone rings…one, two, three, four. Counted, and waited for the answering machine message she had by this time come to expect, idly wondering what nonsense this Devon Burns person might have concocted this time around.

She also wondered, not for the first time, if Devon Burns actually existed, and, if so, was he actually sane? Stupid thoughts—if he didn't exist then Australia's top-rated artist in wood was no more than a myth. Besides, *somebody* had to be in charge of the amazing voice that left messages on her answering machine in response to the messages she left on his.

But if the ways he used a telephone and programmed his answering machine were any indication, she thought, the sanity question was certainly valid. Even the voice, she was beginning to think, must be put on. Surely no human throat could produce such a tone; the gravelly resonance and extraordinary depth suggested that it was mechanically assisted.

'This is Devon Burns's machine,' that hollow-sounding voice intoned. 'My human person is… indisposed just now, leaving me, as usual, to do all the work. If you wish to leave a message, I shall be pleased to relay it at the appropriate time. But if it is truly meaningful dialogue you require, or if communication with a machine is beyond your feeble human

7

capabilities, may I suggest you put *your* machine on the line immediately after the bleep?'

'Damn!'

This was, she thought, the fourth...no, fifth time she had rung Devon Burns, and although each time the message had been different it remained essentially the same—he wasn't there, he would ring back.

And he would, she knew. He always had, every time she had left a message. The problem was his timing, which never, ever coincided with her own. It was almost a week since her first call, and all she had accomplished thus far was a dialogue—far from meaningful—with a machine.

Enough! Damned well enough! Colleen thought frantically, and just managed to be ready when the bleep sounded.

'Greetings, machine,' she intoned. 'This is Colleen Ferrar's machine. Again! *My* human person requires to meet *your* human person...person to person, as it were.'

She struggled to stifle a giggle, then continued. 'As in face to face, in a situation where they might actually be able to communicate in proper *human* fashion. Ineffectual, I realise, by *our* standards, but that is my person's desire, and I would greatly appreciate you relaying that message to *your* person, assuming he actually exists and isn't just a figment of your mechanical imagination.'

Colleen paused momentarily, then let her frustration fuel another foray into the high-tech world of answering machine.

'Fred...surely we know each other well enough by now that I can call you by name?' she said in deliberately sultry tones, her voice dripping with seductiveness. 'The problem is that *my* person wishes to discuss something rather more complicated than just business with *your* person. My human person wishes to discuss art, Fred…as in A-R-T, Fred. Which is something that requires person-to-person *human* contact, Fred, because *everybody* knows that to even *understand* art you must have a soul…and *everybody* knows, Fred, that machines don't *have* souls—*do we*, Fred?'

Colleen took a quick breath and returned her voice again to what she imagined to be that of a mechanical sex symbol.

'Oh, dear, Fred,' she sighed. 'There, I've gone and blown my circuits again. I *do* apologise, but, of course, you know how it is—these human people are just *so* different, so frustrating, so…well, you know.'

And she went on from there, piling it higher and deeper as she freed her imagination, promising Fred the most sensual of mechanical experiences if he would condescend to provide—'at your convenience, of course; I know how busy you must be, keeping your human person functional and artistically productive'— suitable directions so that *her* human person could drive to wherever on Tasmania's Liffey River Devon Burns was located.

'Of course, I will make sure she brings *me* along too,' Colleen continued. 'They will undoubtedly need us, after all, to translate for them if nothing else, won't they? And then, Fred…well…use your imagination…if you've got an imagination, which I frankly doubt,' Colleen added. Then she left her number and hung up the telephone.

She laughed. If it wasn't for the frustration and the diminishing time element involved, she might have enjoyed her experiences with Devon Burns's answering machine a good deal more. But time was running out almost as quickly as her patience.

The first time she had attempted to contact Devon Burns, the machine had told her that he'd been sent to bed without lunch and was not allowed human contact just at the moment. She had laughed, waited for the bleep, then become her own answering machine long enough to leave a brief message asking him to call when his punishment nap was ended.

His reply had come at some time in the small hours, when she had been taking not a nap but a much needed good night's sleep—something, she had thought she'd detected from a note of weariness in that low, growly voice that he could have used himself. Certainly he hadn't been loquacious; he'd merely announced himself, apologised for the lateness of his call and hung up.

From there the whole scenario had become, to Colleen, a black comedy of timing errors and complications. She had emerged from the shower to catch the last words of one message, but hadn't been quite quick enough to grab up the telephone and catch the man himself. She had returned the call immediately, only to be told that *he* was in the bath with his rubber duckie and could not be disturbed.

It must have been a pretty long bath or else he'd drowned; Colleen had waited half an hour, then had had to go and attend to business without getting the expected reply. Subsequently she had tried sweet reason, humour and a dire threat to yank his answering machine's microphone out by the roots. That had got her a brief lecture on telephone manners but had done nothing for the timing of the hoped-for connection.

And now this! Colleen sat staring at her telephone, *willing* Devon Burns to return her call at once. Some people, she knew, used their answering machines to filter and monitor their calls, thus avoiding people whom they didn't want to talk to, but, considering that Burns had always returned her calls eventually, she didn't think he was actively trying to avoid her. Or was he?

It was, she decided, vaguely possible but hardly likely. Devon Burns had the ambiguous reputation of being both a recluse and a womaniser—extremes she personally found quite incompatible and contradictory.

The reclusive aspect might seek to avoid her, but that didn't explain the way he had constantly returned her calls. She didn't concern herself with the womanising side of his reputation; Colleen's interest in Burns had nothing to do with that, however much her machine might try to seduce his. Her interest was in his talent as an artist, not in his looks, his womanising, his masculinity or anything else about him.

'Although I have to admit I *do* rather like your sense of humour…sort of,' she admitted out loud, still staring at the phone. 'And that voice isn't bad either, although I still think it isn't real.'

She got her answer to *that* simply by answering the telephone when it rang.

'Fred?'

Just the one word; no greeting, salutation, hello or other word to prepare her. But it was enough, in that gravelly, deep voice. And, curiously, Colleen had no difficulty at all in figuring out what he meant.

'Of course,' she replied instantly. 'Aren't all telephone answering machines named Fred?'

'Mine,' said the voice, 'is named *Ignatius*. And you've hurt his feelings rather badly, I might add. *Your* machine shouldn't be named Fred either, by the way. What do you call it—Bertha? Or maybe Imogen?'

'Colleen serves the purpose,' Colleen replied briskly. 'Although I don't see why it couldn't be a Fred, unless you have some phobia about sexism among answering machines.'

'I have a phobia about sexism...period,' was the reply, and Colleen fancied that the voice became even deeper than usual. But there was no longer any question about it being mechanically altered, she thought. Or was there? Some sort of distorting device, perhaps. But why?

'Is your voice always that...?' There was no appropriate word to complete her question. What word was there, really, to describe that peculiar resonance, that sensation of gravel being swished around by mighty currents, deep in a seaside cave?

'That...what?'

And she detected a hint of laughter then—deep, hidden laughter, devilish laughter.

'Well, it is a rather unusual voice,' she said, faltering. 'So very...well...deeply pitched and resonant.'

'You don't like it?'

I could listen to it for hours, she thought, but didn't say that; she wouldn't *dare* to say that.

'I...well... I just find it very interesting, that's all,' she finally managed to blurt out. And immediately regretted it. The last thing she wanted was to sound attracted to the man; to have things the other way round would be far, far preferable.

'That's nice,' he said, the voice totally noncommittal now. 'But what I'm interested in just now is what a Colleen machine looks like. I already know what it sounds like, but I find it difficult to get a mental picture. Suppose you could help me out?'

'One answering machine looks pretty much like another,' Colleen replied evasively. But as she looked across her workroom to the wall of mirrors, requisite to her work, she could see quite clearly what *she* looked like; the problem would be to provide Devon Burns with an accurate description. Assuming she would do so, she thought, knowing she wouldn't.

Facing her in the mirror was a small woman in her late twenties, with long, unruly masses of hair shaded from dark brown to dark honey with auburn highlights. Bright blue eyes, a strong nose, wide, mobile mouth, good teeth, deep dimples. Not a bad figure, she reckoned: Very good legs, or so she had been told.

But her own impression had always been of being small, and that the masses of hair threatened to overpower the rest of her diminutive figure. Attractive? Maybe, she thought. But certainly not beautiful.

'If you say so,' was the eventual reply to her cryptic comment, but there was a long silence first that seemed to say far more. 'Ignatius would have preferred more, of course, but he doesn't get that many date offers— blind or otherwise—so I guess he'll manage to live with the disappointment.'

Colleen was uncertain just exactly what was meant by that last word, but even as she was forming the question in her mind Devon Burns continued.

'Mind you, if he went about giving out directions without my permission, he'd be living without a few other things too, so maybe it's for the best, actually.'

'I only needed directions so I could somehow manage to speak to you in person,' Colleen said. 'You needn't make it all sound so...so sinister.'

'I'll decide whether it's sinister or not after you've told me what it is you want,' was the reply. And then, in a whispered aside that she was clearly meant to hear, he continued, 'It's all right, Ignatius, your essential parts are safe—for the moment, anyway.'

'That's a bit heavy,' she bristled. 'What kind of attitude is that to have towards a faithful servant?'

'This is no faithful servant; he's an uppity, high-tech monstrosity who'd run my life into the ground at the slightest provocation. Now let's stop playing around, Colleen...Ferrar. How's about you just state the nature of your business and we'll get on with it, shall we?'

Which caught Colleen rather by surprise. She knew exactly what she wanted from Devon Burns, but suddenly found that to put it into simple words without being able to *show* him what she wanted wasn't as easy as she had imagined. She told him that, faltering a bit in the process.

'*Make* it simple,' was the blunt response, and she could almost *see* him shrug, could feel the coolness of the response. Or at least she imagined she could.

'It really would be much better if I could come and see you, show you—' she began, but got no further.

'Try,' he said, interrupting. And she could sense that he was losing patience with the whole thing.

'All right,' she said hurriedly. 'But it will take some explaining, and since this is your money we're spending here perhaps you'd prefer me to call you back.'

'Now that,' he said, 'is the kind of simplicity I seldom see and do appreciate. Right, you do that.'

And he hung up without another word.

Colleen's temper flickered from amused to near-angry, but she quickly brought it under control as she hurriedly punched out Devon Burns's phone number. It would be just like him, she thought, to have switched on his damned machine and walked out the door; she had best be quick.

'Ignatius,' she muttered with a shake of her curls, and made a face at the woman in her mirrored wall.

But it was not the ubiquitous answering machine that she got after only one ring. It was unquestionably Devon Burns himself, and his attitude clearly hadn't changed much.

'Right. Simple, remember?' he said, without even bothering to say Hello or anything else. For an instant Colleen was struck by the sheer fact of being so easily taken for granted, but she recovered before she began to speak.

'In the simplest possible terms, I have a commission for you—' she began, only to be cut off before she could say any more.

'I don't do commissions.'

'But...but it's not that simple,' she insisted. 'If you'd only give me a chance to explain, or better yet to *show* you what I have in mind—'

'I don't do commissions.'

Blunt, dogged, infuriating.

'There is more to it than that,' she cried. 'Oh...will you just listen—or even just give me the directions to where you are and I'll come out and *show* you?'

'I can't for a moment imagine what you could show me that could change the simple fact that I *don't* do commissions,' he replied.

Right, thought Colleen. Stronger measures were called for here.

'I have,' she said quietly, almost whispering into the telephone in a bid to force him to listen, 'two *enormous* pieces of Huon pine.'

That should lure him in, she thought. Huon pine, a species unique to Tasmania, was a rare wood that was much prized by craftsmen and certain to be in short supply. For an instant she thought that she was on a winner. But then...

'Define enormous.'

'Why don't I just come out and *show*—?'

'Why don't you just do as you're asked?'

Damn the man, she thought. We could go round and round like this all day.

'As big as...well...the size of...'

'Oh, come on...the size of an elephant, a horse, a small dog...which? The size of *you*? Or are you just making this all up as you go along?'

'Certainly not! I mean, really...would I be making it all up at the same time as I am *trying* to find some way to explain it to you?'

'How should I know?' And again she felt that she could actually see the shrug. 'This is your game, Ms Ferrar; I can't be expected to know all the rules.'

'It isn't a matter of rules,' she explained. 'It's just that I can't think of anything I could mention that would give you a proper idea of the size—which is your fault, by the way; if you hadn't suggested anything, I expect I would have come up with something quite easily.'

Devon Burns's laugh was as gravelly and rough as his voice. It fairly thundered through the telephone. But then he just went silent, eventually forcing Colleen to rush into saying something for fear he'd just hang up.

'They're...um...about a metre and a half long by...oh...say a metre across, maybe a bit less,' she finally managed, having to tuck the phone between her ear and shoulder and wave her arms around to judge these very questionable measurements.

Then there was another silence—this one thankfully brief—followed by a low, throaty chuckle.

'If that's what you call enormous, you can't be very

big yourself,' he said. 'Are you absolutely certain you're even grown-up? Maybe I ought to be negotiating with your mother…or your answering machine.'

'I am quite grown-up, thank you very much! But I suppose it has to be admitted I'm not the biggest person in the world. Does that matter?'

'Only in matters of perspective, but we'll let that go for a bit. Am I to assume you have some half-baked plan for me to do something with these enormous pieces of wood…as in something specifically commissioned by you? Is that the idea?'

'Only with one of them,' she said. 'The other one— well, I'm not sure about it. I'm not sure about either one until I can show them to you and see what you think.'

'I think we're both wasting our time,' he said bluntly. 'I don't do commissions, as I've already told you, and two oversized toothpicks of Huon pine don't seem worth risking my privacy for, if you don't mind me saying so.

'Still, if you want to get rid of them, give me your address and I'll stop by for a look one day. If it's decent stuff at a decent price I might take it off your hands, but I have to tell you I far prefer to go and find my own sculpting wood; my needs are really very, very specific.'

Colleen fought back anger. The absolute nerve of the man! Then she thought that if he came to look at the wood, she would at least have a chance to discuss the project she had in mind. A chance to discuss it face to face, moreover! But the timing…

If she couldn't interest him in her project, and soon, there wouldn't be time for him to take it on anyway.

'I really would prefer to bring it to you,' she said.

'And soon. If there's any chance you might take on this commission, I would have to insist on completion by—'

'I've already said that I don't *do* commissions,' he cut in. 'I have quite enough work to keep me busy until I'm ready to retire, which I hope I won't ever do. I also,' he added, with what Colleen heard as a sneer, 'do not work to deadlines—except my own, of course. There is only one person in my young life who insists upon anything, Ms Ferrar, and that is *me*.'

Colleen took a slow, deep breath, fighting for control. Then she forced her voice into submission and said calmly, 'I really do not see, Mr Burns, how it could hurt you to at least *look* at this wood, at least look at what I have in mind. You might even actually decide you *want* to do the sculpture I'm after; I expect it would be very, very challenging.

'And,' she added after a significant pause, 'there's always the question of money. I am quite prepared to pay very well for this, knowing that you are probably the only person who could do what I would like and do it properly.'

'That,' he said, with what could only have been another sneer, 'goes without saying. The question is not whether I could do it properly, it is whether I would do it at all. And money doesn't come into it.'

'Even internationally renowned craftsmen have to eat,' Colleen reminded him. 'Won't you reconsider and at least look at the project?'

'I eat quite well, as a general rule. Well enough that I'm able to pick and choose the work I take on. And just for the record,' he added, 'I like to think of myself as an artist.'

'Well, I think you're being extremely short-sighted about all this,' she replied. 'Only a fool would stand there dithering when opportunity knocks. For all you know this could be the most important project you've ever taken on, and you won't even look at it!'

'Dear Ms Ferrar,' he said then, in the most condescending of tones, 'we don't have a project; you have two pieces of Huon pine and I have work to do. *My* work. If you want me to look at your wood, just give me your address and I'll get there sooner or later and look at it. Otherwise...'

'But *when*? When? Yes, I want you to see this wood, but I also want you to at least *consider* the sculpture I had hoped you might do for me. And the timing is relevant; my father's seventy-fifth birthday is coming up and this is supposed to be his present and—'

'When?'

His voice sliced into her ramblings like a razor, effectively cutting short the torrent of frustration that she was beginning to put into words.

'When what?'

'When is your father's birthday?' he said, speaking slowly, patiently, as if he were speaking to a child. 'The birthday you want this to be a present for...remember?'

She told him, then waited through an aeon of silence before he replied.

'That's five months away. Did you expect this... commission to take *that* long?'

'No, but, as you said yourself, you are an artist,' Colleen said. 'And I might be naïve but it did seem to me that the more time you had in hand the better.'

'Hmm.'

'Does that mean you'll reconsider?' she asked after yet another lengthy silence.

'It means...hmm, that's all,' he replied gruffly.

Another long pause. Colleen wasn't quite so intimi-

dated this time by the ploy; if Devon Burns wanted to
maintain his position as a man not to be pushed it was
fine with her, although it would have been nice, she
thought, to know what he was thinking. It seemed too
ludicrously simple, somehow, to have changed his mind
just by admitting that she had allowed plenty of time
for him to do the commission, but—

'Right,' he said suddenly. 'Got a pencil handy?' And
without waiting for a reply he began dictating a lengthy
ream of directions, starting from the pub at Bracknell.

'I'm not so sure you ought to have done that, old son,'
Burns said to himself after he'd hung up the phone.
'That is one very persuasive woman you're going to be
dealing with, and if her sense of humour is any indication she might prove even more persuasive in the
flesh.'

He reached down idly to scratch at the ruff of the
large, reddish-gold dog at his feet, and received a whuffle of acknowledgement for his effort.

'What do you reckon, my lad?' he asked the dog.
'Did I do the right thing—or have I let myself get led
astray by the promise of all that lovely Huon pine? Pre-
suming it *is* Huon pine, of course. I don't know how
she'd recognise it in the first place, much less where
she could get her hands on such quantities. Worth a
look, though.'

Which, he knew, it definitely was. Good quality Huon
pine, especially in large chunks as described by this
Colleen Ferrar, was never easy to come by, although he
had quite good sources and generally preferred other,
far more visually striking wood for most of his work.
Like the black-heart sassafras in which he was currently
seeking the essence of a siren, a sea-nymph temptress

from various mythologies who lured sailors to their fates. She was there, in the wood; he knew it, could almost see her face, had already found her hair in a swirl of the grain.

'But, we *don't* do commissions, do we, old son?' he asked the red dog. 'We don't, and we're not going to start now.'

Once and only once in his long career had he ever taken on the specific task of creating somebody else's vision from a piece of wood, and although the success he'd achieved was beyond question the ramifications had turned him off ever doing it again.

Burns's strong fingers clenched in the dog's ruff just at the thought of Lucinda, who had modelled for the sculpture. Lucinda—frighteningly beautiful, and even more frightening in the madness that twisted her personality. Lucinda, his distant cousin's wife.

She'd wanted far more from Burns than his artistry, and had been denied as gently as he had been able to manage—which hadn't been gentle enough! And when that very artistry had found her true nature in the wood, revealed it through his then unconscious talent for bringing out such qualities from rare Tasmanian timbers, she had turned upon him with a vengeance born of a quite unstable mind.

'Seven years ago,' he muttered to himself. 'And only now resolved...at least as much as it ever can be, for what that's worth.'

He went to his studio and sat in silent contemplation of the barely started siren—the siren whose face was yet hidden to him, unrevealed in the fine grain of the black-heart sassafras. He would see it, eventually. He knew that. Even knew that it would be a face of great beauty. But now...

'No,' he said, and went outside to work on something else.

All this answering-machine nonsense with Colleen Ferrar had him fascinated, and he was honest enough to admit that as he roamed his woodyard in search of something to occupy the time while he waited for her.

Quite an incredible sense of humour...quirky—perhaps too quirky, he thought. Then he laughed...at himself! She had only been responding to his own approach to modern technology. He could accept the advantages of having an answering machine but something in him still didn't like it. Too impersonal, too remote...until he'd personalised the thing in an irreverent bid to make it at least partly human.

'She picked up on it just right,' he muttered to himself. 'Or else she's a born salesman...saleswoman—which is always possible, I suppose. And there's something familiar about that name, too. Ferrar...'

He searched his memory without success but knew it would come to him in time. Her name wasn't going to be the issue when she arrived, and neither, really, would be her sense of humour.

'No commissions,' he told the red dog at his side. 'You just keep reminding me of that, young Rooster. We don't do commissions!'

CHAPTER TWO

'DAMN, damn, damn...' Colleen muttered the words in a refrain as she pottered along the gulf road out of Liffey, heading west—more or less—in a frustrating attempt to follow Devon Burns's directions. The road itself was no problem, but she was flustered by the speed of events, and his precise mileage directions only complicated things.

'You should be able to make it in less than an hour,' he'd said, then had sternly trampled on her protestations that she couldn't just drop everything and make the journey from Launceston right that very minute.

'Of course you can. You just fling those *enormous* bits of wood into your car, you get into the car with them and you drive to Carrick, then down to Bracknell, and then you follow my instructions very carefully and you'll be here in less than an hour. What could be simpler?'

What, indeed? 'We'll just ignore the lunch I have to cancel, and the two appointments this afternoon, and the fact that I'm busy at *my* work too,' Colleen had muttered—to herself, since Burns had hung up without another word.

She concentrated now on the tripmeter, wondering if it was calibrated the same as Burns's, or if, indeed, she had been deliberately sent on a wild-goose chase. Certainly there was no sign of any form of habitation...and then there was!

But it wasn't much of a sign, merely a rutted, appar-

ently little used track that looked far too difficult for
her low-slung sports car. There was no mailbox, no
sign-post, no gate, no power lines; the track just seemed
to twist upwards from the main road and disappear.

Colleen halted in the road, looked at the track for
some time, then decided that she simply *had* to be
wrong, somehow. Still with half an eye on the tripmeter,
she drove on for another half-kilometre, then that far
again before she found a paddock gateway where she
could turn around.

Even more sure now that she had been deliberately
led astray, she turned into the narrow track and halted,
then got out and began to walk, muttering curses against
Devon Burns as she did so. And to her astonishment,
once she had crested the little rise about fifty metres
along, the track improved as if by magic to become a
proper, small graded road. And from this vantage point
she could see just the tip of a roof protruding from a
grove of trees where the road led.

She returned to the car and drove up the track. The
sports car bucked and churned its way over the first bit,
then settled comfortably on the delightful drive to the
house—which was quite a surprise in itself. It seemed
more to have *grown* on its site than to have been built;
the overall effect was of a structure as natural as the
bushland around it.

Colleen halted the sports car in front of the house,
and turned off the engine to hear, from somewhere at
the rear of the building, the sound of some small motor
screaming in terror or agony. She stepped out and began
making her way round the side of the house, only to
halt and then quickly backtrack as she came face to face
with a large, reddish-coloured dog whose amber eyes
gleamed with malice.

The animal didn't bark, didn't even growl. But by the time she had reached the car it was so close that she couldn't even think of getting inside; there wasn't the time or the space. Colleen backed up tighter and tighter against the car, the dog still holding her gaze with those fearsome, evil eyes as it calmly sat down almost on her toes. And grinned.

A gigantic red tongue drooled across ivory fangs; Colleen could imagine the saliva also dripping on her pale blue silk skirt and ridiculously expensive court shoes, but didn't dare look down to investigate. Then the creature took her right wrist between those fangs and, for the first time, uttered a sound!

It wasn't a growl exactly. More like a moan that rumbled from somewhere deep in the animal's chest, hardly louder than the roaring of her own heart, which threatened to leap from her throat in absolute terror. Then she realised that the dog wasn't trying to bite her, although that in itself was little consolation.

Again it uttered its quaint moan/groan/yodel, this time tugging gently as it stood and started to try and move—with Colleen in tow—around the side of the house where she had originally started to go.

Colleen resisted; the dog stopped, sounded its cry again, then started off with increased determination and a slightly firmer grip—not enough to hurt her, much less puncture the skin, but a grip she dared not even try to break.

'Oh, all right. If you insist,' she found herself saying, and was rewarded by a shortened version of the yodel as the beast stretched its long legs; Colleen almost had to trot to keep up. They rounded the corner, moved along the side of the building, then round another corner. And now, slavering jaws or no, Colleen determined to stop before the monster dragged her right to the feet of the most impressive hunk of manhood she had ever seen.

Devon Burns! It had to be, of course. But the man was so in keeping with that growly, gravelly voice on the telephone that without the dog to hold her Colleen might have had trouble keeping her balance. The dog solved that problem by halting when she did, then sat on her feet without so much as slackening its grip on her wrist.

The man was balanced on a step-stool, only half-turned towards her, his eyes disguised by safety goggles but with the rest of his face clearly revealed. It seemed to be all planes and angles: a jutting jaw, unshavenly dark, a wide, mobile mouth, a nose so strong that to call it a beak seemed almost an understatement, and hair much darker than her own, at least as unruly, and, like the rest of him, strewn with wood chips from the work he'd been doing.

Those shavings were also sprinkled through the coarse mat of chest hair that led from massive shoulders to an improbably tiny waist, but didn't cling to the faded jeans or rugged work boots. As they reached up the man's arms and upper body were corded with muscle— not the bulky muscle of a weightlifter, but the smooth, pliant, whipcord muscles of a natural athlete.

As she watched, transfixed by the unexpected attractiveness of the man she'd come to see, Burns switched off the electrical implement with which he'd been assaulting a massive tree trunk twice his own height and, after holding it well away from his body until it had quit spinning, dropped lightly down from the step-stool and shook the shavings from his hair in a practised motion. Only then, apparently, did he realise Colleen's presence.

It seemed to her to happen in slow motion as he reached up to push the safety goggles away to reveal eyes of the same deep amber as the dog's—eyes that swept up and down and sideways, taking in every inch of her, assessing, evaluating, noting proportion, line, the curve of a hip, the bulge of a breast, the tilt of a chin. They were an artist's eyes, she thought—or a pirate's.

The scrutiny went on and on, Burns apparently oblivious to how uncomfortable Colleen felt at being held there by this gigantic hound while its master assessed her for possible blemishes or…or whatever. And when he finally did speak it wasn't to her but to the damned dog!

'You are a proper *swine* Rooster,' he said with a weary shake of his head, dislodging more wood chips as he did so. Then a broad grin revealed even white teeth as he dropped into a slight crouch and continued speaking to the dog as if Colleen were no more than a duck it had retrieved.

'Well, don't just sit there, you bloody great mongrel,' he said. 'Come on…fetch it here properly.'

That curious growling yodel was almost ear-piercing this time as the great dog lumbered to his feet, dragging the astonished Colleen over to his master, then sitting once again, squarely in front of Burns, and stretching out his muzzle with Colleen's wrist still firmly gripped.

'Leave,' said Burns, reaching down to take her hand as it was promptly released into his own. 'Now go and lie down, you great fool, and pray this woman still has a sense of humour.'

The dog yodelled happily and turned away, but Devon Burns stayed in that semi-crouch, turning Colleen's wrist in his strong fingers, inspecting it in the same way he had inspected the rest of her earlier. Only, now his fingers touched her with equal intensity, and Colleen couldn't ignore the effect. Legs made wobbly on the amazing performance of the dog now threatened to betray her entirely.

'Beautiful,' he murmured, and to her amazement dropped his head to bestow kisses first on her wrist, then the back of her hand and finally, in classic gallantry, upon her fingers. Kisses, she thought, so soft as to be unbelievable—except that she actually saw them happen.

If I were the swooning type I'd be done for, she thought, but any risk of that disappeared as Devon Burns came to his feet, still holding her fingers, and looked down into her eyes, with his own like amber beacons of mirth.

'Not a mark,' he said with a broad, almost mocking grin. 'That dog really has a wonderful mouth, for a Chesapeake. I just hope it stays that soft when he grows up.'

'When he grows up?' Colleen knew that she was squeaking but couldn't help it. Just the thought of that beast being even bigger was enough to drive from her brain the words she had been going to say. At least for the moment.

'He won't get much bigger but he's only a baby, really,' was the curious reply. 'Another year to go, I reckon, before he'll be fully mature.'

Which was just enough to give Colleen's temper a chance to come into its own.

'Well, when he is, I hope he develops a mouth like a dingo trap—and takes *you* in it, for breakfast, lunch and tea!' she snapped, yanking her fingers from Devon

Burns's light grip and stepping back from him. 'It's no more than you deserve, wishing a stupid name like that on a poor, helpless dog!'

She had quite forgotten her own fear at first sight of the huge dog, much less her embarrassment at being delivered to hand like a wounded duck. Colleen was aware only of this strangely compelling man, whose eyes and touch held only warnings for her—warnings she would ignore at her peril.

'If I didn't know better, I'd think you were just a touch cranky, Ms Ferrar. What ever happened to that wondrous sense of humour you possessed?'

'It got lost in the shuffle when that damned hound started dragging me round the yard,' Colleen retorted. 'Especially when all you could be worried about was *his* so-called soft mouth. What about my soft body, for instance?'

'Rooster is a Chesapeake Bay retriever, not a hound,' was the patient reply. 'And your soft body, Ms Ferrar, was never in the slightest danger...from him.' Those incredible amber eyes flashed with laughter as he watched to be sure that she had caught the intent of his final words, then he said, 'Now, come and I'll give you a coffee while I get cleaned up, and then we'll assess this wood you've brought. OK?'

Not OK, Colleen thought. Not one little bit OK—having seen the look in his eyes, having felt the touch of his lips on her wrist. But she meekly followed him into the house, albeit with a cautious look towards the huge red dog that followed them inside.

In the light, spacious and surprisingly tidy kitchen, Burns filled her a cup from a perpetual coffee-machine, plonked milk and sugar on the blackwood table before her and disappeared down the hall, muttering over his shoulder that he wouldn't be long.

Nor was he. Colleen was still sipping her coffee and watching the dog watching her when he returned, hair crisply damp from the shower and that splendid body now clad in clean jeans and a white T-shirt that only served to display his muscles to best advantage.

Having poured his own coffee, he moved fluidly to perch himself across the table from her and lifted his cup in a salute that could have been either polite, mocking, or both.

'I suppose I really should apologise for the rather unconventional welcome,' he said, with a smile that told her that he really didn't suppose any such thing. 'If it's any consolation, that's the first time ever that Rooster has done a thing like that; I have no idea why he did it, but I applaud his taste.'

Mention of his name brought a moan of interest from the dog, who didn't otherwise move except to swipe at those enormous fangs with that enormous tongue. Colleen didn't dignify the charade with any reply at all.

'You're not impressed; I can tell,' Burns said, after waiting patiently for Colleen to speak. 'OK, let's take that as read and get on with our business. Suppose you start from the beginning and tell me about this wondrous wood and this commission you have in mind?'

'Fine,' she replied, glad to be on a firmer footing at last. 'The wood, as you know, is Huon pine, but it's...rather special. My father brought it back from somewhere in the south-west wilderness years and years ago, when I was just a child. His story is that he carried it out miles and miles and miles on an improvised back-pack—he was doing some sort of survey work at the time, I think. He's kept it ever since, or he did until it somehow devolved on me, and it's very, very special to him.'

'Why?'

'Why is it special? Well, because he went to so much effort to get it, I suppose,' she replied. 'He had big plans to do...what you do, I guess. I know he took a couple of adult-education courses in wood carving, sculpture, that sort of thing.'

'But he never got stuck into these two *enormous* bits of wood?'

Colleen paused. Was there a definite look of sarcasm or even just plain disbelief on that rugged face? Whatever, it was gone as quickly as she saw or imagined it.

'He told me once that he was afraid to touch it at first, and when he had learned enough to be able to he said he'd also learned enough to know that he wasn't good enough and never would be, so he left it alone. Does that make sense?'

'Your father sounds like an amazing person,' was the reply, and now the tone seemed totally genuine, even a little impressed. 'There aren't many people with the brains to recognise their own limitations and the integrity to do the right thing because of it.'

'My father is a wonderful man,' Colleen said.

'I'm sure of it. But go on, please. Now we have *you* blessed with two chunks of rare wood, and you've brought them to me; have you got big plans to be a wood sculptor too...or...?'

'Me? Not a chance,' she laughed. 'No, the situation is that, as I mentioned, his seventy-fifth birthday is coming up and he is one of your biggest fans—did I mention that?—and since he is the original man who has everything I wanted to give him something truly special. So I thought if you could do a...what do you call it?...a

bust of him…from one of *his* special pieces of wood…'
She paused, forced herself to meet his eyes directly.
'But I've changed my mind now.'

Those amber eyes flashed a tiny flicker of surprise
and he nodded his head expectantly.

'Well, you've changed it since you got here, I presume. Do I dare ask why?'

'Oh, it's simple. I just realised two things I should
have known all along—my father isn't vain enough to
ever *want* a bust of himself, for starters, and you don't
do carving or sculpture like that anyway. You're famed
for being able to bring out what's already *in* the wood,
or at least what *you* see in it. I'm not surprised, now,
that you got stroppy when I mentioned the word "commission".'

Colleen felt a fool—worse than a fool—at having to
make such an admission, because she herself realised
that she ought to have known better from the very beginning. She had got so wound up in the idea of giving
her father a special, unique present that the realities had
quite been ignored.

She looked at Devon Burns, knowing that if she were
the type to blush she'd be blushing now. She was sad-
dened by the way things had turned out, but accepting.

One dark eyebrow slowly elevated itself, and Colleen
was certain that she saw a cloud of suspicion darken
the amber of his eyes. But when he spoke Devon
Burns's voice gave no such message.

'Certainly an interesting revelation,' he said, rising to
pour them fresh coffee without bothering to ask Colleen
if she wanted more. 'But not surprising, really, except
maybe for the timing.'

'I don't think I understand,' she replied, herself cautious now, even suspicious. His statement had been just a shade too complimentary, and too easily given.

He shrugged. 'Going by your father's reputation as I've heard it, he certainly isn't noted for being vain. If he was, I suspect he'd have had one of those mighty land-development projects named after him, or one of his shopping centres or something. As for the rest...' Another shrug, this one with a slight smile. 'Now that I've finally twigged who *you* are, I'm a bit surprised it took you all this time to realise my attitude about working with other people's ideas; you're an artist yourself, after all.'

Colleen, who had instinctively tensed at being so easily recognised—and had expected a far different remark in the face of it—relaxed slightly. But there was bitterness in her own voice when she replied, and she made no attempt to hide it.

'Thank you...I think. It's nice to find somebody who still thinks so.'

Again that raised eyebrow, but this time his eyes flared with something besides suspicion. Dark amusement? Hostility? It might even have been contempt, she thought.

Whichever, it made it clear enough that Devon Burns might live somewhat isolated but he certainly kept abreast of current affairs. She hadn't been aware that her case had made nearly the splash in the Tasmania media that it had on the mainland, but obviously it had. Unless, of course, he also maintained strong information sources throughout the arts network, which was also likely enough.

'Is that what you're doing in Tassie—licking your wounds?'

'Or giving up? Why don't you ask that too?' she

replied, fighting now to meet his eyes because she had asked herself both questions time and again during the past three months. And not liked the answers.

By the age of twenty-five, Colleen had created for herself a national and international reputation as a clothing designer. And she had done it purely on her own talent and her own money and her own work—hard work and plenty of it. Now, four years later, she considered herself a battle-scarred veteran; she had survived—barely—a vicious and lengthy legal battle over design rights, having been set up by a man she had trusted implicitly...a man she had actually planned to marry.

She'd had her name, reputation and talent dragged through the mud, suffered the pain of betrayal, won the court battle to emerge modestly rich, then sold her label to a multinational to make herself even richer and taken herself off to Tasmania—her father's birthplace—to make a fresh start.

'There's no shame in retiring to regroup,' he said, and his eyes seemed honest enough. 'And it wasn't me that mentioned quitting. As for the rest, well, you did win, after all.'

Win? That had been part of the problem all along for Colleen. She had won in court, had, she supposed, won in selling out for a mammoth price. But she had emerged from the fray so tattered and vulnerable that she didn't feel as if she had won anything at all. Her reputation, to her, would always be in question, and half the industry regarded her selling out to the multinational as just that—a sell-out.

'*Did* I win?' she asked, as much of herself as of Devon Burns, not even realising that she had spoken aloud until she looked up to see the expression in his eyes. It was a question that she couldn't answer and he didn't attempt to.

'Come and show me this damned wood,' he said gruffly. 'After all you've said about it I'm mightily intrigued.' And before Colleen could object he had reached out to take her hand and lift her upright, and, still holding her hand, was moving towards the door.

'But…but there's no sense bothering now,' she said as they stepped outside, with the big red dog almost upsetting her as he shoved past them.

'All the sense in the world,' Burns replied, tugging her in the direction of her car. 'I've heard your story of this wood, and your father's story; I can hardly wait to see if the wood has a story of its own. Besides,' he said with a slow grin as they finally halted by the car, 'Ignatius would never forgive me if I didn't look at it, considering all the effort that's gone into our meeting.'

Colleen had to smile, though she wasn't sure that his still holding her hand didn't also have something to do with it.

Devon Burns hefted the two large Huon pine sections out of the sports car and carried them, one balanced on his shoulder and one under his arm, around to the outdoor workshop behind the house. Colleen followed, admiring the ease with which he managed the task. It had taken all her strength just to roll each piece around the garage floor of her rented Launceston townhouse; getting them into her sports car had been a gargantuan effort.

Burns tipped the section from his shoulder onto a pedestal affair that cranked up and down somewhat like a clothes hoist, and dropped the other piece casually into a nearby sawdust pile, where it landed with a great thud.

Ignoring Colleen now, along with, it seemed, every-thing else but the wood in front of him, he began a lengthy and involved process of inspecting the wood from every possible angle and vantage point. He circled the pedestal with the slow patience of some great hunt-ing cat, moving sometimes so slowly that she could hardly discern it, other times with speed and thrust as he searched for...for what?

Whatever it was, the search seemed to provoke some atavistic, primitive element in the man. His movements became almost a dance, almost a ritual, and she realised suddenly that he was speaking or singing, either to him-self or to the wood itself. There was something quite elemental about the performance; she could recognise no words, but somehow was quite convinced that he was actually communicating.

Ridiculous, she thought. Until he suddenly hefted the log down and replaced it with the other, larger piece of Huon pine, beginning a vaguely similar but somehow quite different performance.

Again it was as if only he and the wood existed in the universe; Burns looked at it with eyes that saw...? Whatever it was, Colleen knew that she could never see it, and nor would anyone else, until Devon Burns's unique skills had brought it out of the wood in his spe-cial form of artistry.

As she watched, entranced, he placed the two huge pieces of wood side by side on a high bench nearby, turning them infinitesimally this way and that then step-ping away to view from first one angle and then another.

Then he moved in close, inspecting each piece of wood by hand, and now Colleen was even more en-tranced. His lean, strong fingers moved over the surface of the wood with a strange intimacy, a caressing gentleness that went far beyond mere touch.

Colleen's skin quivered as she imagined those fingers moving so delicately, so knowingly intimately upon the fabric of her own body. The concept was as exhilarating as it was faintly frightening. Just watching him gave her the shivers; it was as if he could *see* through those sensitive fingers and was viewing the soul of the wood as easily as she could see the outside of it.

And when he finally turned away, shaking himself slightly as if returning from some distant, foreign place, the eyes he turned upon Colleen were more than just amber in colour—they fairly glowed.

'Your father was wiser than I suspect he knew,' Burns said in a voice that was strangely subdued, almost reverent. 'These are superb pieces of wood; I'm not even sure I can bring out the best in them, although I'd surely love to try. You *will* sell them to me, I hope?'

'Sell them?' Colleen was asking that question of herself, not Devon Burns. And somehow the answer didn't fit. Even though she couldn't see whatever it was that *he* saw in the wood, the Huon pine simply was not just a raw material in the sense of bricks or clay or dress fabric. It was that uniqueness that only Burns could see which gave the wood its value, and how to put a price on that?

'I don't know,' she said, moving to where she could put her fingers where his had been, only to find them blind, insensitive. 'I can't see what makes them so special. I simply can't touch this wood like you do and…see.'

'Try.'

That husky voice was near her ear now, and those

fingers had her own encased within them, guiding them to the wood, directing them.

'Close your eyes for a minute and try to let your fingers see the grain, the convolutions in the wood,' he whispered. 'Then look again and see if it doesn't make a difference.'

Colleen tried, but with her eyes closed she was aware only of his fingers upon her own, guiding her, his touch warm, insistent, his breath in her ear even more so. And when she opened her eyes the wood was all out of focus; what she saw was the incredible length of his fingers, the well-kept nails, and she was even *more* aware of his touch and the nearness of him.

She closed her eyes again, and this time she did become aware, but not of the wood. As if a light had been turned on in her mind, she became aware of Devon Burns becoming aware—of her.

The strong, creative fingers that had guided her own were now moving along her wrist, tracing her pulse along towards the softness of her inner elbow. His other hand, on her shoulder, was flexing, the fingers not roaming but gently exploring the texture of her skin beneath the silken blouse.

The sensation was...exquisite. But dangerous—simply too dangerous. Colleen basked in it momentarily, then suddenly straightened up and shifted away from him, blinking rapidly as she found herself staring directly into the sun.

'I'm...I'm sorry,' she found herself saying, not really knowing what she was apologising for, or why.

Burns might not even have noticed her abruptness; he wasn't looking at her but seemed to be concentrating again on the two large chunks of wood. And yet he *had* been aware of her; she had felt it, knew it. But if he now chose to ignore that, well, all the better…because she also intended to.

'You realise I wouldn't have the faintest idea how to go about pricing this wood, assuming, of course, I decided to sell it to you?' she asked.

He grinned, and she saw the devils in his eyes laughing with him.

'I do, if you'd trust me,' he said, and named a price that was low but that Colleen somehow knew was more than the real value as it sat. His grin only broadened when she told him exactly that.

'You're forgetting the delivery fee,' he said. 'Usually I have to spend days, sometimes weeks, searching out exactly the pieces I want; this is the first time ever I've had them brought right to my door.'

Colleen was thinking quickly, hardly paying attention to the attempted gallantry. She hadn't told him, and wouldn't, that the price was really so low as to be irrelevant to her. She'd be as well just to give him the wood and be done with it, she thought, then changed her mind, wondering if…

'What chance is there that you would have either piece sculpted in time for my father's birthday?' she asked.

He shrugged. 'Depends.'

'On what? Have you that much on the go that you couldn't at least try?'

'Oh, I could try. I *would* try, come to that.'

He reached out to the largest of the two pieces, saying, 'The other one is just whispering to me so far, but this one…shouts! But there's a lot between that and producing a finished creation, as I'm sure you realise.'

Colleen nodded. She did realise that; the creative process might be greatly different for him from the way it was for her but there were also definite similarities.

'Would you give me first option to buy it when it's done—assuming that it's finished in time?'

Now it was his turn to pause. She had struck some sort of chord, she realized, but couldn't assess what it was. His eyes had changed, darkened, lost all expression to the point where she couldn't tell if he was angry or just thinking it over.

'Are you really talking about *assuming*…or is that just a backhanded way of putting a deadline on things?'

'I said assuming and I meant assuming. We're not talking about a commission here; I'm only asking for first option to buy *if* it gets finished in time.'

'Not without it going on exhibition,' he finally said. 'I've got a major exhibition coming up—just before your father's birthday, in fact. And another a few months later. It would have to go in one or the other.'

'But if it's already sold—'

'The selling isn't the whole point of the exercise.' And now his voice took on a stern quality; this was Devon Burns the artist speaking out. 'There'd be no sense doing it at all if only one or two people besides me would ever see the result.'

'Well, there wouldn't be much sense either in giving him a birthday present only to take it back again so you could exhibit it,' Colleen replied.

'I don't know why not. Well… I suppose I do, but it isn't the hassle you're thinking it would be. Your father might be quite pleased by such an arrangement.'

'And he might not; my father is a wonderful man, but he has some very, very strange ideas about some things.'

Which caused Devon Burns to say something that

erupted into a coughing fit; unfortunately it seemed to Colleen to have been totally centred around the word 'hereditary'. She scowled at him, but he only cleared his throat once more and returned her scowl with a look of bland innocence that was even more phoney.

Then that look changed too, and now she couldn't read it at all. And Burns obviously wasn't going to enlighten her; he just kept looking, his amber eyes roving her face and hair and body with an apparent idle curiosity that Colleen somehow knew was anything but idle.

There was something in that look which reminded her of the way he had begun to scan and survey the Huon pine logs; his eyes seemed to lose focus slightly, as if he were looking *into* her, not just at the exterior. And it was very, very disconcerting.

Then he shook his head, for all the world as if to clear his vision, and looked over at the logs, then back at her; then he walked round her, and for a fleeting instant Colleen was certain that he intended to reach out and touch her face in the fashion of a blind person but without the manners. Instead, he smiled a gentle little smile to himself, then to her.

'I guess it comes down to the fact that there's only one way to satisfy both of us, and that would be to finish off one of these pieces in time to have it in the exhibition and *then* give it to your father,' he said. 'Assuming, of course, it was a piece you wanted for that purpose. And that you could afford it.'

He softened that last bit with a slow grin, then went on, 'The problem is that it puts me in a very tricky position; I don't like the concept of working to such a deadline...or to such restrictions. It *could*—and I'd be unfair if I didn't warn you about this—stuff up the entire project, because if it goes wrong in my head it'll never come good here.' And he wiggled his fingers expressively.

'I can understand that, I think,' Colleen replied, but cautiously, because he was up to something now and she knew it, but didn't know *what*.

'So one condition would have to be that you don't get to see whatever I'm doing until it's done, whether we make the deadline or not. Nobody else will either, if that's any consolation, because I want to avoid anybody else's vibes, good or bad. The same reasoning makes some writers refuse to talk about work in progress, in case it talks them out of what they instinctively might have done right.'

'Agreed.' Making decisions had never been hard for Colleen; she had learned the art the hard way, over years in a rough business. This one, anyway, was easy.

Devon Burns nodded polite acceptance of her alacrity, then smiled.

'The other condition might be…more difficult,' he said.

'I suppose you expect me to just *give* you the wood?' she suggested, hoping against hope that it could be that simple and having already decided to do that anyway, especially if it gave her a fighting chance to provide her father with the birthday present she wanted for him.

His eyes laughed as he shook his head.

'Nothing as easy as that,' he said, 'especially since you were going to do that anyway.'

Colleen couldn't help but smile.

'You're dangerously sure of yourself. Or don't you know it's very risky to take a woman for granted? Some girls I know would have changed their minds after a comment like that just to be spiteful.'

'True, but I fancy you're not one of them. In fact I

could almost see you agreeing to my second condition sight unseen.'

'Then you're a dreamer and a romantic as well as an artist,' Colleen retorted. 'I didn't come down in the last shower, you know.'

'Not that so much; I just thought since you were so damned determined to make sure you got this present for your father...'

'Go on.'

'No, I'll have to show you,' he said, rising to his feet with the lithe ease of a great cat. 'Come along and we'll see how serious you are about all this.'

Colleen followed him round to the far side of the house, where she was marginally surprised to see what an extensive indoor studio he had created. The structure was a large, octagonal room with a fireplace in the centre and large windows that opened in every facet and matching skylights, to ensure, she presumed, the controlled lighting he required. All the windows had provision for heavy drapes and were screened for summer as well. Despite the fact that several were now open, it was noticeably warmer inside than out.

Burns waved vaguely to a carving bench in one corner, the only obvious seating, then stalked to the other side of the room and gathered a rough-carved wooden figure in his arms so that he could carry it over and place it on a waist-high platform.

'I hope you realise that I don't like talking about work in progress either,' he muttered, not quite meeting Colleen's eyes. 'But in this case...' And he shrugged as if to lessen the sin.

'Then don't,' Colleen insisted, rising to move closer to the life-sized figure. Surprisingly little work had yet been done on it, she saw, but even that was sufficient to begin to show what Burns had seen in the wood itself. It could be nothing else but a mermaid or some sort of sea-nymph, rising from what would become waves. Only the hair had been carved in any detail; the face was still blank, the upper body virtually untouched, and the lower section only roughed out to provide some form of scale.

As she peered at the raw sculpture Devon moved the carving bench over beside the pedestal, and with a rueful smile gestured for Colleen to seat herself once again. The implications were all too obvious.

'You...you want me to pose for this, to model?'

'It needs you,' he said simply. 'It already has your hair; I noticed that when you first arrived. I had to stop there, and now I know why—I was waiting for you.'

'That's...that's ridiculous—' she began, then halted. Not for her to question the logic or lack of it displayed by an artist of this man's calibre. Already she had seen a shadow of something—dismay, anger, a closing-in?—flicker through those amber eyes. It was neither safe nor sensible to say anything further.

They stared at each other, neither ready to speak. Colleen wanted to look again at the fledgling statue but could not free her eyes from Burns's compelling stare. The whole concept of this project having waited for her, she thought, was insane at best. But if it would ensure that he completed her father's birthday present on time...

'Before or after you do my father's present?' she asked, carefully keeping her voice calm, noncommittal.

'During, actually, I suppose,' he said. 'But this one I really want for the exhibition after it, so of course you would have priority; I promised you that anyway.'

'And how often, or how long, or...whatever...would

I be expected to pose? I have my own business to re-build, you know; I couldn't just drop everything and drive out whenever you felt like doing a few moments' work.'

He grinned. 'That isn't the way I usually work any-way. Of course we'd have to look at the logistics. If you're serious, that is; I wouldn't want to get halfway through and have you change your mind just because your father's present was done.'

'I wouldn't do that.'

'OK, but will you do this?'

Colleen thought for a moment, tempted and terrified at the same time. Then she nodded.

'Yes,' she said, and then more firmly, 'Yes. I will.'

His grin reminded her, just for an instant, of the way his dog had looked at her. She could almost imagine the tongue lolling.

'You're here now; want to make a start today?'

'Fine,' she said, feeling nothing of the kind suddenly.

'Good,' he said, turning to pick up a soft pencil. 'Then take your clothes off, please, and we'll get on with it.'

He had to fight to keep a straight face as Colleen's beauty was transformed by a swift series of expressions.

For just an instant, he wished that he could take back the words, but only just for that instant. Then his in-stincts as a game-player took over and he became en-thralled by working out Colleen's reactions, trying to predict what she'd say, how she'd say it...how she would finally decide to cope!

He needed her face. More than needed, he realised—had to have it; hers was the face that was trying to escape from the timber. No question...already the hair he'd completed was her hair, already he could see the first line of her figure in the wood. She was the siren…or would be!

And so beautiful. An unusual beauty, heightened by the underlying strength. He had only a vague memory of the news stories surrounding her court battles, but seeing her in the flesh, talking to her, he could imagine only too well the toll it must have taken, the stresses and strains.

So what do you do? You go and add a few more with your damned silly games, he told himself, still watching Colleen Ferrar, fascinated now by that face, by the resolve behind her eyes.

She was a professional and she knew that he was…she'd sought him out on that basis. And her experiences in the rag trade wouldn't have left her with many hangups about nudity, not that he needed much, really, to complete the siren.

For an instant, a warning flashed across his mind—a vision of Lucinda, her beauty warped by her madness, which had been fuelled by his uncanny ability to draw that very insanity from the timber itself. But he shrugged it off mentally, if not physically.

No, he thought. This wasn't the same…couldn't be the same. And, besides, he needed Colleen Ferrar if he was to get the best from the siren, not that he'd ever quite admit just how much he needed her.

And I'm coming to rather like you too, he thought, looking at her again, silently willing her to accept the challenge, join the game.

CHAPTER THREE

COLLEEN almost bit her tongue in surprise, then almost bit it again as she clamped her jaw shut to prevent herself from babbling.

He must be joking, she thought. He just *had* to be joking. Except...the look in those damned amber eyes said that he wasn't joking at all. Those eyes that seemed to be able to see right through her now seemed to be doing exactly that, moving over her body with studied casualness, disrobing her in the process. Then they returned to meet her startled gaze.

'Problems?' And Devon Burns shrugged, the corners of his mouth lifting in what could have been either a grin or a sneer.

He's enjoying this, she thought, and momentarily hated him for it.

She met his eyes, although she had to force herself to do it. To have him so able to affect her without so much as touching her was maddening. She could feel her tummy churning, all fluttery, and knew that it was a totally involuntary reaction to the man himself.

Her nipples strained against the restraint of her bra, and she knew it was because he somehow managed to touch her with his eyes—a touch as tangible as if he had plucked at her nipples with his fingers...or his lips.

A sane person, she thought, would simply get up and walk out; there were other presents she could get for her father, and to stay here under this man's influence was so obviously dangerous, so foolhardy, but also somehow so deliciously tempting…

In that moment of hindsight it seemed ridiculous not to have realised that he would expect her to pose for the body of the sculpture as well as the face. She hadn't, of course, but that was hardly his fault. And he had, she realised, given her every opportunity to avoid the commitment.

She had no illusions about the propriety of it all—the man was, after all, an artist. Besides, there were far more tempting bodies available than her own—of that she was quite sure. Devon Burns almost certainly had his choice, and, judging by his reputation, he took that choice as often as not. No, she decided, a deal was a deal was a deal…

'No, I don't have any problems,' she finally managed to reply. It was difficult to speak at first, but the respite had gained her control over both tongue and thoughts now. 'It's just that… Damn it—do you really expect me to take off all my clothes in front of that bloody dog?'

Burns's laughter was a booming, roaring gust of fresh air through the studio; it was as if he had suddenly thrust open all the windows, all the skylights. He looked at the red dog, suddenly alert at the noise, then looked at Colleen, who was slightly taken aback by his reaction, and then he laughed again, even louder.

But when he spoke it was to the dog rather than Colleen.

'Well, my old lad…consider yourself told,' he said. 'And here I thought *I* was the dirty old man. But she's right, you know—if you start developing a taste for tender young maidens, Lord knows what you'll bring home next.'

He ushered the dog to the door, shooed him outside,

then turned back to stare at Colleen through eyes still alight with humour.

'Right, then. You've disrupted my privacy, corrupted the tender young mind of my dog, tried to seduce my answering machine...what other tricks have you got up your sleeves, Ms Ferrar?'

'Only an arm or two,' she replied, attempting to match the apparent lightness of his mood. Then she began, slowly and quite deliberately, to unbutton her blouse. 'And not even that in a minute. I suppose it would be silly of me to ask you just how *much* you expect me to take off?'

'You can stop right there,' he replied, voice gruff now, almost, she thought, edging into anger. 'I was only stirring you a bit, as I suspect you knew very well; the time will come, obviously, when you'll have to reveal all for the sake of my art, but for now I'm more interested in your face than the rest of you—pleasant as I'm sure it is.'

Colleen paused with her fingers on the lowest button, so surprised at his remark that she wasn't sure that she'd heard aright. And, although she did her best to hide it and was fairly certain that she had succeeded, she was grateful beyond belief for the reprieve. Immediate hindsight made her wonder what sort of insanely dangerous game she had been playing; vanity made her wonder at Burns's refusal to continue it.

He was staring at her again, holding the pencil to his lips and touching the end of it with his tongue, his eyes out of focus again. What did he see? she wondered. He was looking at her, and yet somehow he wasn't; he was seeing into her, or through her, or...something.

Moving over to the supine, partially carved figure, he made a few markings, then directed Colleen to look one way, then another, then up, then down, all the while making what seemed to her to be more mental observations than markings on the wood.

But in his close attention he offered her a wonderfully unique opportunity to observe him as closely as he did her, and she took every advantage. The intent concentration furrowed his brow, giving those eyes an even more predatory look that was only enhanced by the great, beaky nose. And it seemed as if he talked silently to himself as he worked; every so often his teeth would bare in something approaching a smile, and she found herself wondering what errant thought had created the gesture.

And those hands! Long, lean fingers, obvious in their strength, moving with a sureness and delicacy of touch that belied their size. There wasn't a thing about him that didn't somehow fit that overall impression of alertness, of being superfit, poised for immediate action or reaction.

He was like a great, predatory animal, so quick and decisive in his movements that he made even his big dog look slow and clumsy.

And he loved the wood he worked with. It was clear in his every movement, in his very expression as his eyes moved from herself to the figure he was working on, she thought. Even as the pencil in one hand swept out to mark some effect he wanted his other hand didn't just hold the figure steady, it actually seemed to caress it, to seek some communion with the grain, the texture, the very essence of the wood.

For a moment Colleen couldn't help but let her imagination wander; she closed her eyes and let her mind feel those grateful fingers stroking her as they did the figure for which she modelled.

She wasn't totally inexperienced with men, although she had spent so much time and energy building her career that there had been little time for them. Except for Andrew, of course, and she didn't—wouldn't—let herself think of him. But somehow she knew that this man—this strange-eyed, predatory man with the artist's fingers and eagle's eyes—was different, was like nobody she had ever met, certainly like nobody she had ever been *touched* by.

In her mind she envied the statue he was working on, idly wondering if the wood could somehow appreciate his touch, the attention, the genuine *feeling* he had for it. Empathy, she thought. And envied even more.

She disappeared into her own mind, lost in daydreams of Devon Burns as a lover, his strong fingers caressing her. Without ever having known it, she could feel his touch on her breasts, across the flatness of her tummy, down the softness of her inner thighs. Her lips moved, moulding themselves to his kiss; her fingers clenched, mentally experiencing the coarse texture of his dark hair, the flowing lines of his whipcord muscles.

She could feel his breath warm against her skin, hear him whispering her name, breathing it out in tones that no one had ever used before—tones of passion, knowing, longing...

'You can stop now. Or come up for air at least.'

The voice was the same, yet different. Now those gravelly tones held a note of sour amusement that effectively ruined the aura of her daydream. And when she opened her eyes to look at him there was a similar note in the expression of his amber eyes.

'Lucky bloke...the one you were dreaming about.'

'How did you know...?' She paused then, struggling to hide her feelings, to retreat from what she thought must be obvious in her eyes. To have him realise that *he* was the subject of her daydreams would be humiliating in the extreme.

He merely shrugged, showing no sign that he had twigged onto her thoughts. 'Whatever you were up to, it sure didn't seem to be any sort of nightmare,' he finally said, and again there was the hint of amusement in his eyes and voice.

'Hardly surprising, since I wasn't asleep,' she replied, not sure if she ought to be miffed by his assumption or not.

'Oh, I don't know. It isn't always necessary to be asleep to have nightmares…or erotic fantasies.' And his eyes flashed now with what could only be mockery.

Colleen bristled. 'Is that what this—' she pointed to the sculpture '—is supposed to be? Some sort of erotic fantasy in wood? I can't imagine that many people would want to pay your prices just to stimulate their juvenile imaginations.'

The amber eyes narrowed, first angrily, then in something closer to speculation.

'That,' he said, 'will become a siren, as in mythology. If there is any erotic element—and there damned well better be—it won't be for the purpose of stimulating juvenile imaginations, Ms Ferrar. It will be to illustrate the very essence of femininity—calculated attraction based upon even more calculated deceit.'

He paused, eyes flickering from the statue to Colleen. Then he continued, 'The wood, by the way, is blackheart sassafras. A particularly fitting choice, wouldn't you say?'

'I would say you're bordering on becoming a misogynist, if you're not there already,' Colleen retorted.

'If you dislike women so much, why bother to carve one at all?'

'I don't have a choice,' he replied. 'There is a siren in that chunk of sassafras and it's my role to bring it out for the world to see. I can't turn it into something it's not.'

'But why a siren? I accept, I guess, that it has to be a feminine figure—even I can see that—but couldn't it be a madonna, or just a simple, uncomplicated mermaid?'

'A mermaid is still just a siren; same legend—different name. And as for a madonna…well, you've only to touch this piece of wood to know that it wouldn't work. There's a sort of…voluptuousness about it, a sensuousness that certainly doesn't lend itself to simplistic elements of purity and goodness.'

'Which is no compliment to your choice of model,' she said. 'What does it all make me?'

'Said she who goes about trying to seduce poor, innocent answering machines just to get what she wants.'

And his eyes fairly glowed. The look he was giving her, Colleen decided, neither answered her question nor even tried to; misogynist or not, there was definite seduction in those eyes, and, what was more, she was meant to see it.

'I did *not* attempt to seduce your damned answering machine,' she replied. 'That was *my* answering machine that did that, and well you know it. I personally wouldn't stoop to anything quite so…so…'

'Mechanical? Or should we say electronic?'

'I was going to say calculating and deceptive,' she snapped. 'It's more than a bit possible that machines, given half a chance, could have better human qualities than some humans. But then, I suppose that wouldn't ever have occurred to you.'

She was starting to get angry now, and didn't really want to. Colleen shifted round to slide down from the carving bench, suddenly aware that half her bottom had gone to sleep; as her feet hit the floor she stumbled and would have fallen had not Devon Burns swooped forward to catch her in his arms.

Once caught, she was held; he made no attempt to release her or even to slacken the encircling band of his strong, muscular arms. Instead, he held her close against him—so close that she could feel the beat of his body against her, could look up and see the amber highlights of his eyes from a proximity closer than she might have preferred.

'Speaking of machines,' he murmured in a low, throaty voice, 'Ignatius had this message he wanted passed along to Bertha or whatever her name is. I presume you wouldn't mind taking it with you.'

'Wha—?'

She got no further, and her mind was still pondering what foolishness this infuriating man could be about now, when his mouth dropped to cover hers, his lips forceful, almost punishing as they forced open her mouth to accept his kisses. His arms seemed to crush the breath from her, and so unexpected was his passionate assault that Colleen had no defence, no ready armour.

When his fingers began to orchestrate a response, playing her spinal column like some sensual keyboard, she could only sag in his arms, her mind objecting but her body already conquered. When his tongue probed between her lips they opened to his kisses like the petals of a flower seeking the sun, revelling in the taste of him, the texture of his mouth.

But it was his hands that so completely defeated her. As he lifted her against him her blouse pulled out from the waistband of her skirt, allowing access to fingers not work-roughened, not hard and calloused and brutal, but so sensitive, so knowing as they frolicked over her bared skin that it was like being tickled by feathers, caressed by wind-driven flower petals.

And then, as quickly as it had begun, it was over. Those sensitive, strong hands put her aside like a discarded tool, and the amber eyes, when they met her own, were cool, distant, with no sign in them of the passions he had roused in Colleen herself.

'You'll be wanting to get back now, I expect,' he said, as if they had just finished a cup of tea. 'And I have work to do.'

Five minutes later she was driving back down the road, aware that her blouse was still not tucked in, aware also that her mind was even more thoroughly rumpled. She had been expertly dismissed, whisked away like a pesky pedlar whose wares were unsatisfactory or, worse, unwanted.

'Here's your hat; what's your hurry?' she muttered, far more angry in retrospect than she had managed to be at the time. Even when Burns had been kissing her, taking total control of her body and emotions with an ease that was frightening, she hadn't really been angry; now she was.

'Damn it! Nobody should be able to do that,' she growled, still more aware than she wanted to admit of the touch of his fingers on her skin, his lips on her mouth. The reality had been far more intense than her earlier daydream had been able to suggest; the man's sheer masculinity, his deliberate expertise had touched depths in Colleen's own passions that she hadn't quite expected.

It was sobering—and maddening—to realise that he had controlled the entire experience. Had he wanted to take her, right there on the workshop floor, he could have done so and she would have let him. She knew that now, and even if she hadn't at the time, *he* had, which made it all the worse.

And it was far from over. She knew that too and was both angry and confused by it. She had made a bargain and now had no real choice but to follow through on it. Unless she turned around this very minute and drove back there, unless she could renege, and do so before he had a chance so much as to *touch* her father's wood, she was committed; sooner or later she would find herself having to take her clothes off to pose for his sculpture, would find herself exposed to the control of a man who didn't even like her.

Her mood was thoroughly black by the time she reached her rented townhouse, which unaccountably now looked somewhat bleak and sinister after the wonderfully nature-integrated setting of Devon Burns's place.

Entering the lounge, which she used as a workroom, she flung her handbag into one chair and herself into another, glowering at her reflection in the wall of mirrors across the large work table.

'You're a fool, Colleen,' she muttered. 'Nothing but a damned...silly...fool. All this, just to get one of Devon bloody Burns's sculptures for Dad...and you don't know what it will end up like or whether you'll even *like* it, much less whether he will.'

She was still muttering when she glanced over to see the red light on her answering machine flashing.

'OK, Bertha, or whatever your name is,' she growled, but went immediately to review what messages might be there, because she was a self-confessed victim of telephone technology. If a telephone rang during working hours, Colleen believed that it had to be answered—a throwback from her days on the mainland, where the phone had been such a vital part of her business day.

Indeed, it had only been since her move to Launceston that she had managed to restrict herself to having only one telephone, and that in the workroom; at bedtime she turned off the bell and let the answering machine do the work while she slept. It had been necessary when she'd first arrived because her number had kept getting all sorts of mistaken calls that had wakened her every night for the first fortnight.

It might be nice to be like Devon Burns, she thought. He seemed to have taken just the opposite tack—he ignored his telephone entirely when he was working. 'And he's probably too busy at night to answer it anyway,' she muttered as she moved across the room to check her own machine.

First, a message from her father, who lapsed into an office mentality occasionally, despite his retirement years ago, and wondered now why Colleen wasn't at work in the middle of the day. Then her mother, who thought because she wasn't there in the middle of the day that she must be working...perhaps too hard? And then, that impossible, improbable voice...

'Ignatius here. Art thou well, Bertha...or is it Imogen? No matter—"a rose by any other name..." et cetera, et cetera, and a very curvaceous bit of circuitry too, I fancy. One day, perchance, we could...

Well…perhaps now is not the time for such dalliance. I but relay a message to your human person, who should arrive any moment now…'

Colleen could hardly believe her ears, had to replay the message again to be sure she had actually heard aright.

'My human person wishes to make it known there is a rather splendid production of *A Bedfull of Foreigners* at the Princess Theatre this week, and if *your* human person fancies dinner and the theatre could she a) have you let me know absolutely soonest, and b) please trundle down and get tickets for same. Friday night, if you please, and *decent* seating, if you please—not in the ashtrays. Oh, and my human person will arrange for dinner. Assuming this to be agreeable, please advise your person to dress appropriately—as in wear legs—and provide me with an address where she will be collected at six p.m. sharp.'

'I'll give you six p.m. sharp,' Colleen cried, and grabbed up her telephone to begin punching out Devon Burns's number as if she were trying to drive the buttons through the phone. But as she reached the last number a modicum of sense took control and she slammed the receiver down without completing the call.

Burns, she had just realised, almost certainly wouldn't answer the telephone himself anyway; he'd made it abundantly clear that he considered his telephone a servant for his own convenience and only used it for outbound calls, especially during working hours. So she would be dealing with his insane alter ego Ignatius, and for that a little preparation was in order.

Ignatius! Just the thought of that name forced a splutter of laughter, but it was nowhere near enough to dampen her anger and astonishment at the overall turn of events.

'The absolute nerve of the man! First he leads me down the garden path about the wood, then he kisses me stupid, then he gives me the royal heave-ho. And now…this! What a ridiculous, absolutely asinine way to go about things!'

It was an ardent, passionate speech indeed, but she noticed that the scowling reflection in the mirror wall didn't seem overly impressed.

Colleen sat there for long moments, staring first at her reflection then at the silent telephone, which crouched there like a cat waiting to pounce.

Her first reaction was simply to phone him back and tell him what to do, but that, she quickly decided, was too extreme, and hardly realistic if she was going to fulfil her commitment and get what she wanted out of this insanity. But to stay involved, especially on Burns's own terms, was very, very dangerous. She would stay involved—but *she* would set the terms, Colleen decided. Just how was another question!

First things first, she thought, and reached out for a pencil and paper. First, the proper response from…? Clearly she must find an appropriate name for *her* answering machine if she was to enter fully into Burns's little game, even if it was only to be for this once.

'Freda! If all male answering machines—except of course Ignatius—are named *Fred*, then a female one must be Freda. Good, that's that little bit out of the way. Now…'

It took her half an hour of writing, rewriting and more rewriting but finally she was satisfied with the first part of her plan, even if the rest was no more than a hazy intent to get even, one way or another.

But by this time her mood had improved immensely; it was good fun, actually, orchestrating an overheated, flamboyant dialogue of sexual innuendo between two machines. She dialled Burns's number, then waited with bated breath for the proper response. If he answered himself, she realised at the last instant, she would have to hang up immediately. But if things went as she expected...

And they did. She was dutifully informed that Ignatius's human person was recuperating under a 'very long, very cold shower' after what he described as a 'truly harrowing experience' earlier in the day.

'One for me,' she chuckled as the message rambled on. And when it was her turn she was more than ready!

'Ignatius, darling,' she began, dropping her voice into what she hoped was a sultry if machine-like tone. Then she went into it with a vengeance, first disposing of the business at hand. Of course her human person would get tickets for the theatre; she would be instructed to rush out immediately if not sooner to get the very best seats still available. She provided her address, confirmed the time, affirmed that yes, legs would be worn. 'Although why I simply cannot imagine, darling; I hardly ever wear them myself...so inadequate, really, when one has the availability of much sexier and more useful optic fibres, don't you think?'

At the finish she got so carried away that she had to fight to keep the laughter from escaping into her voice. She did manage, in the end, to sign off with the smooch-iest kiss she could impart to the phone.

'So much for you, Ignatius,' she said after hanging up. 'And I hope it sends *you* to the cold showers too. Now for your illustrious master...'

Her plotting and scheming in that direction lasted

through the next three days, during which she obtained the tickets for the show as requested, then pondered and fussed and nearly drove herself crazy trying to determine how best to put the handsome, irreverent Mr Burns in his place.

She wandered past the theatre on the opening night and was dismayed to find that only a small proportion of the audience bothered to dress up at all. The next night was from a fashion point of view even worse. Launceston people quite obviously didn't get terribly excited about dressing up for the theatre.

'But *I'm* expected to,' she said to herself. 'Which indicates that *he* will too. Unless, of course, he turns up in work boots and a bush shirt, with that damned dog in tow. Which wouldn't surprise me in the slightest, although I suppose it's unfair to say so.'

But it wasn't. Not really. Devon Burns was so totally unpredictable, so completely irreverent and self-contained that just about anything, she thought, was possible where he was concerned. The problem, which only seemed to become more and more unresolvable as Friday evening drew closer, was what *she* was going to wear!

'Legs, legs, legs.' She was humming the words in a toneless dirge at five o'clock on Friday, with only an hour to go and no more ideas of how she would dress than she'd had two days earlier.

She had decided on and discarded a variety of options from all over the fashion spectrum, and indeed almost settled on one or two vague possibilities. The concept of wild tartan tights with a slinky checked miniskirt and a striped top was suitably outrageous, but her natural good taste balked at the very thought. She looked at

thigh-high boots, at tights in every conceivable pattern
and style, long skirts, short skirts, miniskirts—the lot.

And the problem really was, she had determined at
this next to last minute, that she refused to compromise
her own taste just for the questionable effect of stirring
some reaction from Devon Burns.

And her taste, really, was essentially simple and un-
cluttered. She had made her name with design that held
its style and value in a market that changed with every
passing breeze, and she just could not flaunt herself in
some ridiculous outfit even for this very worthy cause.

'When in doubt, simplify!' she told herself firmly at
five to six, all made up but so far dressed only in her
skin and fast running out of time and options. When the
doorbell rang two minutes later she was slithering into
a deceptively simple, *very* short evening dress in classic
emerald-green, fumbling to try and get both shoes on
as she made her way to answer it.

To hell with it all, she was thinking. If he wanted
legs, then legs he would have. Legs, and plenty of bare
arm, back and cleavage into the bargain; this simple
short gown with its cross-the-throat halter-neck left
very, very little to the imagination.

And Devon Burns's reaction to it, she was delighted
and also somehow relieved to find, left absolutely *nothing* to the imagination. He looked at her as she opened
the door, his eyes roving with undisguised pleasure
from her rowdy hair to the pointy tips of the shoes that
gained her a full three inches of height. Hardly enough
to matter, in some ways, given that he was still five
inches taller, but every little bit helps, she thought.

His smile was startlingly bright against the darkness
of his tan, as was the white dress shirt he wore beneath
a dark suit that could only have been custom tailored.

The overall effect, Colleen thought, was nothing short of stunning; if Burns had been impressive in snug-fitting work jeans, he was even more so dressed appropriately for a night out.

Colleen had a momentary flash of the tartan/check/stripe combination that she had considered wearing and silently blessed her common sense, though she did let slip a smile about it. The smile broadened when Devon proffered a paper-wrapped bottle.

'For the house,' he said simply, adding a tiny bow to make the gift somehow even more official.

Colleen invited him in after being assured that they had time for a brief drink and that they could, in fact, walk to dinner and then the theatre if she so wished; the evening was splendidly mild and certain to remain that way.

She felt a momentary pang of alarm as she led him into her workroom—and looked it. Somehow it had simply not occurred to her that she would be forced to entertain this man or any other here, and the revelation was a surprise.

But Devon appeared nonchalant; he strolled around, looking at her sketches, while she retreated to the tiny kitchen to mix their drinks. And when she returned he looked at her!

'Call me a chauvinist if you like,' he said with a slow grin, 'but that outfit is quite simply stunning. Your work, obviously.'

'Obviously?'

'I would have thought so. It has everything I would have expected from you; let's put it that way. Style, simplicity, tastefulness...' And he shrugged to imply whatever else.

'Thank you, I think,' she replied. 'It does make things

slightly…difficult when a girl is advised only to "wear legs"; you might tell Ignatius that for future reference.'

Devon's eyes roamed across her body like a horde of Mongol warriors before he replied.

'He's only a machine, after all, and they do have their limitations. Anyway…' he lifted his drink in salute '…if we drink to your very good taste, it will surely prosper.'

And he did so, thereby forcing Colleen to follow suit.

A few minutes later they started off to walk to town—a decision Colleen almost regretted, as she said, when they passed what just *had* to be Burns's car. It was one of the now rare Volvo sports models, but from the look of it in perfect condition.

'It's a classic,' she enthused. 'I am suitably envious.'

'It's closer to being an antique, like me,' was the surprising reply. 'But you have my promise of a ride later, if you want it.'

There was some satisfaction in the way passers-by looked at them, not least after Devon took her hand when a youth spinning around the block in his car almost collected Colleen in the process. He continued to hold her hand as they went along, and it added something…interesting to the experience, she thought.

When he subsequently guided her into one of the many entrances to Yorktown Square, Colleen began to wonder which of the wide choice of restaurants he had booked at—not because she particularly cared but purely out of curiosity about the man himself and his taste.

So when it became obvious that they were headed for the extravagant hotel which backed onto the square, she felt just a pang of disappointment, having secretly expected a less conventional choice. But the feeling was short-lived, quickly replaced by a sense of total astonishment when she realised Devon Burns's true dining intentions!

passed a too-thin-and-hand concert hall cloak, top was short over, sickly, followed by a sheet of total drenching when she rushed. Devon Burns's too difficult imagination.

CHAPTER FOUR

COLLEEN peered across the dome of a gigantic Ballarat Gold Digger ice-cream sundae, idly wondering at the mentality of a man who would demand that a girl get exquisitely dressed up for a dinner and the theatre, then, with a choice of half a dozen restaurants, including Italian and Japanese, take her to eat at an *ice-cream parlour*. And to look so damned smug about it! She honestly didn't know whether to laugh or cry or throw something at him.

Devon Burns slouched indolently in a plastic chair across a plastic table from her, totally comfortable, it seemed, despite the incongruous paper bib which covered the front of his evening suit. Mustard clung like an errant smear of yellow lipstick at one corner of that incredibly mobile mouth, and even as she watched his tongue shot out to flick away the mustard and those amber eyes laughed as he caught her staring.

'This is the only place I know where I can get better hot dogs than I can make myself,' he'd said as he'd held open the door for her. He'd laughed, and she with him, because it had somehow just fit, somehow been just about what she might have expected, in a peculiar way.

Colleen thought he should look ridiculous, so why didn't he? She had even willed herself into half believing it, but only half. He was too totally in control and too obviously enjoying himself for that description to fit properly. For herself, she thought, ridiculous might

66

actually be an understatement; she not only felt that way, but was certain that she must look it, since she too was wearing one of the huge paper bibs.

And she was not impressed!

They weren't talking; talk had been virtually impossible since their arrival at The Australian Ice Cream Parlour, mostly because the upstairs floor was the scene of a children's birthday party, attended, she was certain, by a *zillion* screaming, riotous rug-rats. It was little short of pandemonium, making it difficult enough even to think, much less carry on any sort of intelligent conversation. Not, she noticed, that it seemed in the least to bother Burns, or the staff, who seemed oblivious to the racket as they paraded back and forth with trays of hot dogs and impossibly exotic ice-cream treats for the screaming hordes above.

The proprietress, a dumpling of a woman with a smile like a lighthouse beacon, had greeted Burns like an old friend and grinned hugely when he'd pointed to his own chest and then Colleen's while mouthing the word 'bib'. She had seemed quite used to taking instructions and orders via sign language at such times and her staff were equally up to the task.

Devon and Colleen, seated beneath what she privately thought must be the epicentre of the chaos upstairs, had used similar sign language to determine their choices from the variety of hot dogs, tacos, nachos and multi-flavoured ice-cream products—more than thirty flavours, according to the menu, and Colleen hadn't doubted it for an instant.

But she hadn't expected her companion, having already quite astonished her—and most deliberately—by his choice of venue, then to make a fair stab at working his way through the lengthy list of speciality hot dogs,

grinning all the while like the child he must once have
been. And, she thought, perhaps still was!

She was still marvelling at that, along with the truly
gigantic sundae that had arrived with her own and
which he was eyeing hungrily when the party upstairs
ended with a cheer and a roar and children, seemingly
by the hundreds, began to stream down the staircase and
out of the door, accompanied by a straggle of parents
whose haggard expressions told a tale of their own.

But it wasn't this exodus which caught her attention—that would have gone relatively unnoticed—it
was the last departing child, clearly the birthday boy. A
slender, beautifully proportioned child, he descended
the staircase almost as a conqueror, amber eyes sweep-
ing the room below as if to say, Look at me! Look at
me! I'm special.

Amber eyes! They hardly registered in her mind, then
she glanced from the boy to Devon Burns and back
again, her mind suddenly aflutter, hardly able to credit
what she was seeing. And as she looked back at the boy
she could only marvel at his resemblance to Burns—
surely, unquestionably, the man he would eventually
grow to be, in appearance if nothing else.

The lad made a faltering step at the bottom of the
stairs, his entire demeanour altered, his attention visibly
focused on Devon, his amber eyes alight, a curious expression forming on a mouth the exact miniature of
Devon's.

It wasn't, Colleen realised with some surprise, recognition. Not as such. The boy wasn't looking at Devon
as an individual, a person he knew. But she was certain
beyond all logic that she was seeing something that was
like recognition—a drawing of type to type, perhaps.

Then Colleen heard—felt?—a single word as it

snapped like a whiplash from somewhere above, drowning in an instant the look on the boy's face, wiping the colour from his eyes to leave them blank, closed, shuttered.

The sound which had so affected the boy had been meaningless to Colleen, but from the periphery of her attention she caught the impression that Devon Burns had suddenly become aware of the lad and that *he* recognised the sound, the voice, the word instantly!

She slowly turned her head to make sure and followed his gaze as it flowed like a laser beam between him and the boy. It was incredible to watch—a tangible, visible link between his eyes and the boy's. Then Burns's eyes lifted, and she followed that glance too, immediately aware of the coldness in it, the icy blankness as he focused on the figure that was descending the staircase, behind the boy.

Burns's eyes seemed to pale, and the amber highlights dimmed to a dull glow the colour of light ale, although colder than any ale could be without freezing. There was no visible emotion—neither surprise nor anger nor rage—only a pale, icy bleakness that was of itself even harder for Colleen to contemplate.

The figure descended; first the long, long, shapely legs, followed by a feminine shape so lush, so almost *over*ripe as to seem a parody. Then an unquestionably beautiful face framed by a wild mane of hair the colour of fire. Too vivid to be natural, yet somehow also too vivid to be anything but, Colleen found herself thinking.

And the eyes! Enormous, vivid, like pools of darkest chocolate but—as they met those of Devon Burns—without a hint of chocolate sweetness. They were eyes alive with malignant emotion—crazy, savage eyes that focused on Burns with a strange, almost unreal intensity. Never had Colleen seen so much malevolence expressed that way.

Burns seemed not to notice, or else, she thought, was totally inured to the sensation. He met the woman's eyes steadily, bleakly for an instant, then turned his gaze again upon the boy as the woman's hand reached down to clench at the child's shoulder.

Whether she was holding the boy back or holding herself upright was difficult to determine. Her slim fingers clenched so tightly that the boy squirmed with the pain, tried to twist from her grasp and finally managed to do so. But he didn't then attempt to move toward their table, as Colleen had half expected he might; instead he managed only one fragile step before halting, his shoulders slumped in acceptance but his eyes still locked with Burns's, assessing him, memorising him, Colleen thought, as if Devon Burns was some rare thing he'd never seen before.

Colleen returned her attention to the woman, who stood in unmoving silence, still trying to kill Devon Burns with those chocolate-coloured eyes.

She was, Colleen decided, a truly striking creature by any definition, with a vibrant, wild beauty that could neither be denied nor diminished by the other immediate impression which she radiated, which was one of...cheapness.

Colleen felt an inner shudder as that word sprang to mind, but it was, she decided upon reflection, the one which most accurately described the distinctly feral aura that this woman exuded—an almost feline wildness. Everything about her was just that shade off centre, the dress a touch too tight, too short, just subtly the wrong colour to match that flaming hair.

Feral, but so vibrant, so vividly alive. Small wonder,

Colleen thought, that she might have drawn such an equally vivid man as Devon Burns into...into what?

She swung her eyes back to where man and boy remained in some silent communion, and realized that only a moment had passed, though it seemed like hours. In Burns's eyes, as he regarded the boy, was a most strange expression—something akin to the way he had looked at Colleen's pieces of rare Huon pine; in the boy's eyes was...something she couldn't interpret, and for neither of them, it seemed, were there words for any other communication...only this strange, strained silence that was almost unnerving to observe.

The boy seemed about to reach out, then something in his eyes changed, as if he'd lost interest. He turned and moved through the door, not looking back. The woman—surely his mother?—shot one more acid glare at Devon Burns, widened it fractionally to include Colleen herself—or did she imagine that? she wondered immediately—then followed. Burns watched them go, the expression on his face unreadable but far from pleasant.

Colleen also watched them go, unable to keep from wondering what lay behind the scenario she had just witnessed. The red-haired woman was, she decided, a truly impressive specimen. There was something about her though—something quite indescribable but also quite obvious, something...not quite right.

But the worst part for Colleen was that she suddenly found herself seeing mental pictures of Devon Burns with this woman—close to her, touching her, making...love with her... She shook her head to try and drive away the unexpected, unwelcome visions, which touched her consciousness like a bad smell.

But it was little use; with her eyes open the images

persisted in her mind, and when she closed them again
it was to remember that lean, muscular body leaning
over *her* at the carving bench, the touch of those strong,
uniquely talented hands, the flavour of his breath when
he'd kissed her. Madness, she thought, but a madness
that seemed unwilling to go away.

She opened her eyes again, looked down to see her
ice-cream sundae still a mountain, still awaiting her
spoon, and found herself wondering why it hadn't
melted in the raw fire of the emotions around it.

'We can be off to the theatre whenever you're ready.
But don't rush; we've lots of time. I'm just going to
slip over to the loo first.'

Burns's voice and demeanour now revealed nothing
of the tensions and emotions that Colleen had just witnessed; it was as if the entire episode had been no more
than a figment of her imagination. She looked at him,
her eyes narrowing in speculation, almost in wonder.
How, she thought, could he so quickly, so casually dismiss what had clearly been a traumatic and emotional
situation for him? And now, with it over and done, was
he not going to offer *any* explanation?

'Well, I'm damned if I'm going to *ask* for one,' she
muttered to his departing back. 'It's none of my business in the first place. I'm not really interested, and I
don't really think I want to know anyway!'

Which was more than half a lie and she knew it, even
admitted it, if only to herself. The difficult part now
would be keeping her tongue and her curiosity suitably
separated; if she didn't watch herself she'd be asking
him anyway, without thinking and almost certainly
bluntly, to explain something that she knew in her soul
was best left *not* explained.

He returned a few minutes later, sliding his lean

frame into the chair across from her and resuming the assault upon his own ice-cream sundae with a studied, somehow sensual nonchalance, devouring the ice cream with his lips, tongue and teeth but all the time devouring Colleen with those damned amber eyes.

She had seen something similar in a movie once, and for the briefest of instants was inclined to dismiss this performance for exactly that—a glib and carefully orchestrated performance. Except that it worked!

Burns's eyes touched at her left earlobe as his tongue caressed the vestige of ice cream in his spoon, and she could almost *feel* the warmth of his tongue against her ear. When he breathed against a fresh spoonful as if to further cool it—how insane! the thought—she could *hear* his sigh, *feel* his breath against her throat.

As his eyes moved around her face and body, caressing, touching, Colleen tried her best to resist the ploy, but even her boldest, fiercest glares had no effect except to draw an equally bold, almost challenging grin.

'I do wish you'd give it a rest,' she finally had to say, her own ice-cream sundae finally beginning to slump; she didn't—couldn't—eat it, didn't care to put such a chilly substance against the fluttering of her tummy.

'Give what a rest?' he asked, eyes now radiating an innocence that she doubted he had *ever* possessed.

'All the deep, meaningful, soulful looks,' she replied sternly. 'Goodness...next you'll be swooning at my feet or something.'

'Men,' he said round a deep-throated chuckle, 'do not swoon. Not even under provocation.'

'You're being deliberately provocative yourself,' Colleen retorted. 'Although why I cannot imagine for the life of me.'

'You're quite amazing,' was the equally amazing reply, followed by a silence that cried out for, demanded an answer.

'I can't see why,' she finally replied, 'unless you think it's amazing that I can't eat ice cream in the quantities you seem to manage.'

Not even the grace to look sheepish! He merely grinned more widely, openly laughing at her now.

'That isn't what I mean and you know it,' he finally said. 'I was referring to your extremely unfeminine lack of curiosity.'

'You've got your concepts mixed up,' she replied, cautious now, keeping a tight curb on her tongue. 'It's cats that are famous for curiosity, and *they* don't have to be feminine.'

Again that wolfish grin, along with a barely perceptible narrowing of those amber eyes.

'Cats find curiosity a terminal illness,' he corrected her. 'Women, in my experience, merely find it among the most satisfying of stimulations.'

'Well then, I hardly envy you your experience,' Colleen retorted.

'Which means?'

Colleen could only shrug. She didn't dare let him lead her on this track; the dangers were all too obvious—at least to her.

Burns sat there a moment, his eyes unreadable, his smile now distinctly predatory.

'Which means you know exactly what I mean and choose to pretend you don't,' he finally said, the grin disappearing in the process. 'Which, as I said, I find amazing.'

Colleen almost sighed audibly in relief. Maybe now he would drop the whole thing, stop his probing.

Fat chance!

'So you're not even going to ask what that wondrous performance was all about,' he mused. 'Hardly an unreasonable question, I would have thought. Perfectly logical one, actually…'

'And absolutely none of my business,' Colleen blurted out as he paused. Then she snapped her mouth shut and stared down at the remains of her sundae, willing her tongue to freeze solid and never, ever work again.

One dark eyebrow shot up in what was almost certainly mock surprise; the amber eyes took on a curious fire.

'If Lucinda hadn't been in such a good mood it might have been your business,' he said then, spitting out the name like a bad taste. 'She has been known to produce some unholy scenes, with incredible embarrassment for all concerned—except herself, of course. I don't think anything would serve to embarrass *her*.'

'But it was nothing to do with me,' Colleen said, genuinely confused. Surely the situation she had witnessed had involved only Burns and the fire-haired woman, and would have been little different without her presence? Or *had* she been included in that final visual assault? And, if so, then why?

'And damned lucky for her she realised it,' he growled savagely, replying, she realised, not really to her but to some inner voice…

The following silence was thicker than ice cream. And colder. But not, thankfully, as long-lasting. Colleen made sure of that!

'All right, I give in,' she said with a scowl. 'I'll play your little game…under protest. So let's have it—who was the lady and what's it all about?'

Devon smiled, but it was a smile devoid of warmth, and when he replied his attempt at humour was too bleak, too black to really work.

'Well, I'm *not* about to say, That was no lady; that was my wife—you can bet on that. Although I dare say the first half mightn't be far off the mark. I'm just pleased Lucinda didn't stage one of her...performances for your benefit, that's all.'

'Performances? I don't think I quite understand.'

'Just as well too,' he said, with a hint of a chuckle that seemed surprisingly genuine. 'Let's just say the last time I encountered her in a...public situation she created a scene that was highly embarrassing both for me and the lady I was with. I wouldn't like to even imagine you *wearing* your sundae, and I'm sure you'd prefer a different image yourself.'

'Very definitely. Though I can hardly imagine you putting up with such nonsense,' Colleen replied almost without thinking, but on immediate reflection could quite understand his meaning when he raised an eyebrow and replied.

'What would you expect me to do? Add to her pleasure by laying a nuisance charge or returning the assault, or...?' He shrugged. 'I generally make it a policy to avoid her, but—as tonight—sometimes luck doesn't work that way.'

He shrugged, almost but not quite casually. 'Lucinda—' again she couldn't help noticing the way he spat out the word '—doesn't always row with both oars in the water. She's more to be pitied than censured, I suppose, but it's damned hard sometimes.'

'You're saying she's...' Colleen couldn't quite bring out the word 'insane' '...disturbed?'

'There's a proper technical term for it,' he replied.

'Somewhere between manic-depressive and compulsive-obsessive, I think. When she takes her medication and the world goes right for her she can be nice as pie, or so I'm led to believe. But other times…well…'

'And this was one of the *other* times? I mean..?'

'*I* am what constitutes the other times, at least too often for comfort,' he replied. 'This evening was better than usual, probably because the boy was involved. Whatever else, she can't be faulted as a mother; again, so I'm told.'

Then he shook his head as if to whip away bad memories like droplets of water from his hair.

'Look, let's just leave it there, OK? It's a long and complicated and rather dreary tale, actually; it doesn't make decent table talk and it isn't conducive to the enjoyment of good theatre either. We had comedy planned tonight, not melodrama.'

Which, Colleen realised, explained everything and absolutely nothing. Who was Lucinda, that he couldn't even utter her name without it emerging tainted from his lips? And who was the child so like Devon Burns as to make *that* question almost ridiculous? And…

'But why——?' She bit off the question, mentally shaking her head at her own stupidity. She didn't need to know, didn't *want* to know—except, of course, that she did.

Some expression flickered across Burns's face, but so quickly that she might have been mistaken. He looked down at the empty sundae glass before him—whatever else, the incident hadn't blunted *his* appetite—then sighed deeply and looked up at her with eyes that danced icily.

'Because…' he said, and his voice was even colder than his eyes. 'Because darling Lucinda believes exactly

what I'm sure *you* believe, my dear Ms Ferrar. She believes that I am that boy's father!'

And there he stopped, letting the statement fall to the
table between them like a well of ice. But his eyes continued the statement, challenging, provoking, demanding some response from her.

'What *I* believe?' Anger boiled up now—anger
caused by the immediate flush of guilt at the accuracy
of his comment. In truth she wasn't absolutely certain
what she believed, but the evidence, at least on the surface, was fairly damning, she thought. The boy was his
spitting image; the mother surely had *some* reason for
her obvious hatred of Devon Burns, and...

Colleen did her best to hold back her tongue but it
was too late.

'I think you're getting just a bit carried away, *Mr*
Burns,' she retorted. 'A *lot* carried away, in fact. I can't
see why I should believe anything...or anybody—you,
her, whoever! It's none of my business for starters and,
for your information, I couldn't care less!'

'Ah,' he said softly, but his eyes said far, far more.
They cast her lie back in her face; he didn't need to
mouth the words.

Then he grinned—a broad grin that didn't touch his
eyes.

'No sense either confirming or denying it, then,' he
said. 'So I won't bother. Time we were away, I think.'

And he was on his feet, a hand extended to help her
up, before Colleen could think. Only when she was on
her feet, had been gently turned round so that he could
remove her bib with fingers that grazed tantalisingly at
the nape of her neck, did she realise how adroitly she
was being manoeuvred.

She shrugged off his touch, though the feel of his

fingers remained on her bare shoulders even as she stalked through the doorway ahead of him, unsure for a moment if she was going to stay with him or search for a cab and give up the entire evening as some sort of bad joke.

The cool evening air brought a breath of sanity, and despite her better judgement she slowed then to let him catch up, and matched his pace as he crossed the square and turned up a narrow alleyway to their left.

Devon Burns didn't try to take Colleen's hand as they made the short journey from the ice-cream parlour to the Princess Theatre, not even when they jaywalked across Brisbane Street to the theatre's entrance.

She'd probably break my arm or chew my hand off at the wrist, he thought. If looks really could kill I'd be a dead man twice over tonight for sure. Damn Lucinda anyway, he thought with a sudden surge of anger, then thought again, and thanked his lucky stars for whatever he'd done so right that he'd deserved finding Lucinda in one of her less provocative moods! Damn yourself... It would make more sense, if there *was* any sense to all of this.

He had only thought of taking Colleen to the ice-cream parlour as a lark, and was forced to admit to himself at least a modicum of surprise at how quickly, unexpectedly the whole thing had come off the rails.

Not the first time my so-called sense of humour has got me in trouble, he mused, at the same time glancing sideways in frank appreciation of the beautiful woman walking beside him. But this time...well, blackmailing her into posing for him had been an impulsive gesture immediately regretted—but not quite so much that he was ready to admit it and retract. Not yet, at least—although tonight was to have been a sort of beginning.

He'd been certain that she would accept 'dinner' at the ice-cream parlour in the spirit in which it had been intended, and he was equally certain now that she had, at least at the beginning. Which was wonderful; it confirmed his first impression that she was not only a fascinating woman but that she had a properly balanced sense of humour into the bargain.

Not that it needed confirming, he thought; anybody who could cope with the introduction that Rooster had given Colleen Ferrar could manage almost anything. And the games she'd played with his answering machine…well…a strange way to begin a relationship, but certainly effective.

But it had all changed now. Explaining Lucinda—and, more importantly, her son—was not going to be an easy task, although it should have been—would have been if he hadn't let himself be carried away with the dramatic approach, if he'd just calmly told her the facts and let them speak for themselves.

Colleen Ferrar was neither blind nor stupid; she had clearly noticed the family resemblance and jumped to the obvious conclusions, or was at least headed that way.

Simple enough to explain, he thought. Just not easy. Especially given that, for whatever reasons, he wanted—would have wanted—to make such an explanation to this particular woman at the right time, under the right circumstances, using just the right words.

Well, you blew that one, my lad, he thought as they sat through the comedy like two strangers in adjoining seats, both laughing in the right places, at the right times, but never really *together*.

And then they walked the long, long walk back to Colleen's unit, still like strangers, not talking, neither of them even trying to recapture whatever rapport they'd started with.

They said their obligatory farewells like strangers, and Devon Burns walked to his car in an unseasonal chill, shaking his head at the stupidity of it all—*his* stupidity.

'Like a blind date gone wrong,' he muttered as he started the long drive back to Liffey, then laughed bitterly. He had never had a blind date in his life and seriously doubted if Colleen had either.

Colleen marched straight from front door to bathroom, shedding clothing as she went, conscious only of some inner need to try and wash away the bad taste of the whole thing. It wasn't until she lay in bed, restless and sure that she would never sleep, that Devon Burns's caustic remarks began to revolve in her memory like a poor-quality tape recording.

'She believes that I am that boy's father!' he'd said. Colleen mentally rewound, listened again. 'She *believes*...' 'She *believes*...'

'How stupid!' she cried. 'What did he mean, "She *believes*"? Surely she'd either know or she wouldn't? What was she, I wonder—asleep at the time?'

The more obvious explanation—that he might have been one among many—flickered into consciousness only to be instantly discarded. Whatever else, she knew instinctively that that was *not* Devon Burns's style and never had been, not even the six or so years ago when it would have happened. No, she thought, never... never...never!

But how, then, to explain the extraordinary resemblance? And, more curiously, the fact that she was somehow certain that Devon Burns had never seen that child before tonight?

'He hadn't; I'm positive of it,' she muttered to herself. 'But he *knew* about him; he as much as admitted that!'

She eventually drifted off into an uneasy sleep—a sleep haunted by chocolate eyes that hated and amber eyes that did nothing but confuse and confound her.

CHAPTER FIVE

'To PHONE, or not to phone: that is the question.'

Colleen repeated the crude parody of Shakespeare, scowling at herself in the mirror as she did so and wishing that the question was as easy to answer as to pose.

Three weeks had elapsed since what she tried humorously to term the 'cold-dog' episode—three weeks in which she had debated regularly whether to try and reach Devon Burns by telephone or not.

'Not! Definitely not,' she told herself for the umpteenth time. 'I don't care what the glossy mags say is fitting for the modern girl to do—I'm damned well not going to call him first and that's that!'

Which drew nothing but a puzzled response from her image, along with the comment, 'But this is business; you're not phoning for a date, for goodness' sake.'

Business it might be, but considering her part of that business involved posing nude for his damned mermaid, or siren, or whatever it might turn out to be, Colleen found herself at a definite psychological disadvantage. If *she* phoned first, it would have the effect of increasing his power in the situation. But what if she didn't, and if he had already decided to abandon the entire agreement in view of their chilly parting...?

'Well, I guess I'd just have to find another birthday present for Dad,' she muttered. 'Hardly a crisis, that.'

Then she chuckled at herself, half expecting that mirror image to grow a liar's nose like Pinocchio, admitting to herself that the real issue here had very little to do with business.

Devon Burns still had a clear four months in which to complete—if he was going to—whatever sculpture he chose from the Huon pine she had given him, and she knew instinctively somehow that, having promised, he would do his best.

'But will he still expect me to keep my side of the bargain?' she asked the mirror, not for the first time during the three weeks. The answers hadn't been encouraging. One day she would be convinced that he wouldn't bother, the next day she'd be positive that he'd enforce the bargain to the letter.

The real problem was deciding—no, she thought, 'admitting' was the better word for it—which option she really honestly wanted. Admitting it to herself, at least; she wouldn't dream of admitting it to Devon Burns.

The fact that he hadn't phoned did not help. The fact that virtually nobody else had phoned either made it even worse.

'I give you a proper name, Freda, and see what happens?' she growled at the silent answering machine. 'You get all uppity and neglect your work. No, I suppose that isn't quite fair; maybe you're just in love.'

A sobering thought, and one that on immediate reflection she preferred to discard.

The weather was generally less than helpful into the bargain. It had rained at least a little bit every single day since his chilly departure from her doorstep. Today was no exception, adding to the forecasts for major flooding of rivers throughout north-eastern Tasmania. Commentators were dredging up ancient flood records and speculating wildly about the one this spell of rain would create.

Colleen found most of their calculations difficult to follow; since her arrival in Launceston the trip to Devon Burns's property had been the longest she'd made, and her memory told her that there had been a fair number of bridges involved. There was an idea about the Liffey running into the Meander, which always seemed to get a mention in the flood reports, and the Meander running into...was it the Macquarie or the South Esk? She didn't even have a proper map, and that lack suddenly, inexplicably, began to bother her.

'You'll take any excuse to get out of working when it isn't going well,' she accused the image in the mirror, deliberately attempting to ignore the fact that her work hadn't been going all that well for nearly three weeks and she knew exactly what the reason was. A quick check of the telephone directory, and five minutes later she was out of the door and splashing happily through the puddles *en route* to the TASMAP offices in Civic Square.

An hour later she was back, loaded up with maps and touristy pamphlets, all of which landed in a heap on her work table when she entered the flat to find Freda's single red eye winking incessantly, absolutely demanding that she push the message button. Which of course she did, but not without first having to conquer an unexpected and surprisingly strong tremor of apprehension. It could be anyone leaving that message, she thought, but *knew* it was Devon Burns.

'Ignatius here,' said the unmistakable voice. 'It is now Friday: ten forty-three a.m. precisely. In approximately one hour, if the weather holds, a rather waterlogged human person might be expected to knock upon your door begging to trade lunch somewhere *very posh* for an hour of your valuable time, to be spent posing for what he euphemistically terms *sketching*.

'You've heard of it, I'm sure—a lot of lines and doodles signifying absolutely nothing in orderly, technological terms but apparently satisfying to the human psyche. If not, I am certain your delightful Freda will be pleased to explain. Should this bargain be acceptable to Your Reverence, that is. The shortness of notice is, of course, duly apologised for.

'I am requested to say that should this prove at all inconvenient you are quite at liberty to send the earlier mentioned human person packing without bothering about explanations, et cetera, et cetera. Being a human person of rather pedestrian gastronomic taste, he could undoubtedly be sent to the local hot-dog shop or milk bar with no risk of any stain upon your pristine conscience.

'There is obviously no logic in attempting to contact this wayward human through my august services today,' the voice continued, and Colleen fancied that 'Ignatius' must by this time be struggling to keep from hysterics; *she* was! 'But, of course, I am always open to the blandishments of the buxom and bounteous Freda, whose synapses positively overwhelm my poor self. Oh! Let me hie myself to the cold shower just at the mere thought lest my circuits explode...'

The wail which ended the message echoed one from Colleen as she looked at the clock to see that the predicted arrival of Ignatius's human person was imminent and that she was hardly dressed appropriately.

'Or am I?' she mused, peering into the work mirror. An aged, weary sweatshirt with both elbows missing...jeans that fitted like a second skin but had less elasticity—one knee was gone and the other on the same downhill skid, and both legs were soaked almost to the knees from her playing in the puddles...sneakers in worse shape than the jeans and at least as wet...

Add her distinctly unfashionable coat, Colleen thought. Forget about make-up, throw away the comb— her hair was already in a rough ponytail— 'And you'll do,' she told the image. 'You'll do just splendidly, thank you, and the posher the restaurant the better!'

The image joined in her roar of laughter and then the doorbell rang.

Devon Burns was hardly what she would have called waterlogged. Ravishingly, devilishly handsome, Colleen thought, was a far better description. He was respectably dressed for a *very posh* lunch, too.

And, damn his amber eyes, he was also too fast on his feet mentally, waterlogged or not. One dark eyebrow flickered upwards and back again as he looked her over, so quickly that Colleen couldn't be absolutely certain she'd actually seen it, and the only other hint of reaction was a slight quirk of that mobile mouth just as he began to speak.

'Ah, you got the message and you're all ready—and on time too,' he said with well-feigned delight. 'But I shall have to speak to Ignatius about this, Ms Ferrar. I did distinctly ask him to advise you there was no need to get all gussied up,' he said, devils laughing in his eyes. 'Still, it would be a shame to waste such a... fashion statement. Good thing I've booked at somewhere it will be properly appreciated.'

First round to you, Colleen thought, but was careful to keep her reply appropriate despite a sudden lurching, fluttery feeling in her tummy. This had all the makings of a great plan gone wrong before it even started!

Here was Burns, nearly as gorgeous in a conventional

business suit as he'd been in evening clothes the last time she'd seen him, and there she was looking like death warmed over—and the rotter didn't even turn a hair!

Worse, having given her outlandish costume a mere cursory glance, he now focused those damned, omniscient eyes on her own, almost challenging her to further indiscretion.

'Probably Freda got it wrong somehow,' she finally managed to say. 'She's only a girl, after all, and likely got all flustered merely *speaking* to someone of Ignatius's stature.'

Which gained her what she hoped was a genuine grin. It looked genuine anyway, although with this infuriating man it was impossible to be certain.

'Undoubtedly. He's a rum 'n, that Ignatius. He wants flogging—but help is damned hard to come by these days, as I'm sure you know,' was the reply, given with a nod that conceded at least a draw for Round Two.

He helped her on with her raincoat, treating it like some luxurious fur, then took her elbow and escorted her to the kerb, where a mud-streaked, hard-used four-wheel-drive dual-cab utility waited like a tired, patient horse.

'Ignatius, the blighter, probably forgot to warn you about the vehicle problem,' he growled. 'But with the flooding and all…well…it would be nice to be able to get home from here, even if it means taking the long way round.'

Ignatius also hadn't warned her about the passenger! As Devon handed her into the high-set machine a great red rug heaved itself up from the rear floor and, with a ghastly moan, tried to lave slobbery kisses all over her neck.

'Rooster! Go and lie down, you great oaf,' Burns shouted over Colleen's shoulder. The dog obeyed, after a fashion, as its master walked round to seat himself behind the wheel.

'Fool of a dog, you might have ruined the lady's posh outfit,' he said, and for Colleen the only consolation was that he seemed to be fighting to maintain his composure.

'I do apologise, but unfortunately the damned dog's smitten. There's no other word for it and nothing, I fear, to be done about it. He's reached *that* age, you know. But perhaps it's only puppy love and he'll get over it in time, poor chap.'

And Round Three to you on points, Colleen thought, struggling now to hold back a giggle. But what she said was, 'He may, but will I? Oh, Rooster…you're a darling, really you are!' And she turned to throw an arm round the big dog's neck so that she could try and hide the sound of her laughter against his rippling coat and beneath his moans of canine ecstasy.

Round Four, she lost, blatantly—at least in her own estimation—when they strolled into Dee and Mee, arguably one of the state's finest restaurants and highly reputed even at the national level, and nobody so much as batted an eye at her hideous costume! Not the staff, not the other diners, all of them respectably—some elegantly—dressed, already seated for luncheon. Not so much as a single raised eyebrow!

Not fair, she thought; a place of this quality has more important priorities than mere fashion, and besides, I'd give ten bob each way he's so well-known here he could have brought *Rooster* and nobody would say a word.

Which, of course, was at least partially true; from the first moment it became clear that Devon Burns was well-known and well liked in the restaurant, and clearly an old and valued customer. If he wanted to arrive with somebody dressed as if she'd just stepped out of a dumptruck, well…

He had known it would be this way, too. Not that he would so much as hint at that by word or gesture. But he'd known! His eyes admitted it—those all-seeing amber eyes with the devils dancing in them; devils that laughed, too, as Colleen was seated across from him.

Why couldn't they have given us a less conspicuous table? she thought, suddenly regretting very much the impulsiveness of her rash attempt to get even with him for getting her all dressed up and then taking her to the ice-cream parlour.

He was *supposed* to be embarrassed by her outfit, supposed to see the humour in it, though—even if there wasn't any. And she was beginning to think that there wasn't, at least from her own point of view. Burns, however, was clearly enjoying himself, and Colleen suspected that she'd end up paying for this lunch in one way or another, almost certainly to her regret.

This particular restaurant had been high on her list of 'must do when I get time' priorities, but now she found herself wondering if she could ever muster the courage to visit the place again. Not that I suppose they'd recognise me anyway, properly dressed, she thought, and was genuinely thankful that she wasn't in Sydney, where *somebody* she knew would have been certain to turn up as witness to this ridiculous flight of fancy.

'How do you feel about a drop of Pipers Brook chardonnay?' Burns asked, and had to repeat the question because Colleen was so far into her own head that she didn't hear the question first time round. She nodded absently, still half-lost in her own thoughts.

'Or would you prefer some cordial?' he said then. 'I suppose you realise you look about sixteen in that outfit; I'd hate to be accused of corrupting the morals of a minor.'

Colleen could only glare at him; there was no appropriate answer, any more than there was to his next remark.

'And I do wish you'd try to relax a bit. This isn't like your in places over in the big smoke, you realise. Here people come for the food—which is damn well worth it—not just to be *seen*.'

'Just as well,' she muttered, speaking more to herself than to him, and mentally conceded defeat. Devon Burns had been a step ahead all the way along, so she might as well relax and enjoy what the menu suggested could be a truly memorable meal.

Which it was! Everything she had was innovative in concept, perfectly prepared and stimulating to the palate—so much so that Colleen was comfortably able to use the meal to dominate the conversation, avoiding anything more intimate. It wasn't until the coffee stage, by which time she'd almost forgotten her embarrassing appearance, that she looked up to meet Devon's speculative glance, to hear him slowly drawl, 'You look happier now. Your mood comfy enough to handle modelling for me for an hour or two?'

'I was until you asked,' she replied, her voice surprisingly calm considering the swarm of butterflies that had erupted from the pit of her stomach in response to his question.

One eyebrow shot up, then he chuckled softly, the sound much more gentle than the speculative gleam in those damned amber eyes.

'You're not harbouring some ridiculous fantasy that

I'm going to somehow compromise you?' he asked, his look turning from speculative to downright provocative. 'Or throw you into a pile of sawdust and ravish you?'

And his eyes wandered down her cheek to touch at her neck, to graze blatantly on the hillocks of her breasts in a gesture so deliberate, so calculated, yet so damned effective that she could actually feel the caresses.

'A bit tricky, that, since I was planning to do this first bit of sketching at your place, and I doubt you've got such a thing as a great heap of sawdust on call.'

'I'm quite certain that you're a dedicated professional,' Colleen replied evasively, wishing that she believed it, knowing that she didn't want to—not completely. He was quite capable of ravishing her with his eyes alone.

'That,' he replied, 'was never in question. Which doesn't explain why you're being so evasive.'

'Maybe I'm just a coward,' she replied.

'Now you're being ridiculous.'

'Probably because I *feel* ridiculous,' she muttered, once again all too conscious of the way she looked, knowing that it wasn't his fault but quite prepared to blame him for it anyway.

'Best *you* finish off this bottle of splendid wine, then,' he said, not rising to the bait either by agreeing with her or by lying and contradicting her. 'It might help you to be a little more relaxed about it all.'

'I won't *need* relaxing,' she snapped, unreasonably cranky and not really sure just why. 'I'll keep *my* side of your damned bargain; you needn't worry about that.'

'I never doubted it for a moment. But I would like to have some feeling that you weren't looking at this as if it was a trip to the dentist.'

Then he chuckled before adding, 'Although in terms

of sheer boredom I suspect modelling might be even worse. I can't say for sure personally, of course, never having tried it myself.'

'If that's supposed to reassure me, it isn't working,' Colleen said, reaching out to pour the last of the wine into her glass. She gulped it down with indecent haste, then started to her feet. 'Right...let's get on with it before I chicken out entirely,' she said.

The courage lasted until they were home, only to disappear the instant they were inside the flat and Devon had seated himself in the workroom, sketch pad in hand and half a dozen pencils carefully laid out on the coffee-table beside him.

'I...well...what exactly do you want me to do?' Colleen found herself saying, barely able to speak for the trembling that seemed to emanate from the very pit of her stomach. She'd been telling herself all the way home that these feelings were quite ridiculous, that of course Devon Burns was a professional, that she was being nothing short of plain silly. But she herself wasn't buying it.

Devon's grin was both wicked and mischievous, neither of which helped. He laid down the sketch pad and walked over to look down into Colleen's eyes, the grin expanding as he did so.

'In a minute,' he said gently, 'I'm going to be sitting there, where I was, carefully *not* looking, since it seems to worry you so much. What I'd like you to do is this...'

And he walked over to seat himself on the sofa, his back to the chair in which he had been slouched, his right arm draped over the back of the sofa, the other clasped round an upright knee.

'Just sit here like this...that's all there is to it. Of course, it would help considerably if you took your jumper off first, since my siren isn't to be wearing one and the whole point of the exercise is to sketch the naked back that will be hers.'

Then he was on his feet and standing close in front of her again, only somehow she hadn't even noticed him move. And he was too close, his hands reaching out to take her shoulders and draw her towards him.

'Settle down, Colleen,' he said softly. 'You really are overreacting, you know, and if you don't stop it you'll be all tense and repressed and it'll show up in the musculature of the sculpture and make a bloody great mess of the whole thing, and then I'll be cranky and you'll be cranky and this will all be a massive great waste of time for both of us, so let's just get on with it because I haven't got all day and I don't expect you have either. OK?'

Dipping his head, he dropped a brief kiss on her forehead—a kiss so light that he might almost have aimed to miss; a moment later he had turned away and was seated, stoically inspecting his array of pencils and muttering quietly to himself in words that she couldn't hear.

He was also, she was certain, smiling to himself, enjoying her discomfort as much as she was *not* enjoying it. Colleen took a single deep breath, then flung off the sweatshirt and scampered across the workroom to position herself as directed, damning herself for a coward and Devon Burns for the chuckle that she was certain accompanied her move.

But then there was only silence, though it was a strange silence that seemed to reverberate loud as thunder in the room. Colleen could hear it over the booming of her own pulse in her ears as she held the pose that Devon had asked of her, and waited...

And waited...and waited. The silence grew louder,

but now, over it, through it, she could hear, or thought she could, the sound of Burns's breathing. No sound of pencil on paper, no sound of movement from the man behind her—just the faint whisper of inhalation and exhalation, broken occasionally by what seemed to be a sigh. It went on and on, finally becoming too much for her ragged nerves.

'What are you doing?' She whispered, but her voice sounded louder than a whisper; it seemed to thunder in the room.

'I'm waiting for you to relax,' said a calm, quiet voice. 'There's no sense sketching you when you're all strung out like this; I wouldn't get the effect I want.'

He paused; she had no reply. The booming silence resumed, her tension fairly crackling through it, not diminishing as he wanted, but growing as if in response to having been mentioned.

Colleen stared down the length of the sofa, her eyes roaming across the fabric, along the end-table, up the flowing shape of the lamp it held, noting a smudge that accused her of slackness in her most recent bout of housecleaning, then, even worse, spotting a wisp of cobweb in the corner of the room.

A sigh. Then another, this one heavier. 'I don't suppose you smoke,' he said.

'Certainly not,' she replied. And then, with a sigh of her own, went on, 'I must admit that for the first time ever I almost wish I did, if it would help me get through this.'

'It might help you relax.'

'I don't *need* to relax,' she insisted, knowing that she lied, able herself now to feel the tension in her shoulders, the strain on the arm she leaned upon. 'What I need is for you to get busy with your sketching and get it over with.'

'Close your eyes,' he said then, and Colleen obeyed, only to snap them open again in alarm as she felt him sit down behind her, felt his hands close on her shoulders, his thumbs meeting on the top bone of her spine, heard him say, 'Now close them again and trust me. I'm not here to hurt you; I'd never want to hurt you. I just want to ease some of this tenseness out of you.'

The words overrode her gasp of surprise. The fingers—those strong, sensitive, artist's fingers—were already kneading the tense muscles along the base of her neck, with a touch that was at once impersonal and all too personal for her to ignore.

'Trust me.' The phrase echoed over and over as Colleen gave herself up to the magic of his massage, allowing her body to slump sideways against the back of the sofa and forwards against her knee.

His massage was neither gentle nor harsh, but it was unquestionably knowing, his touch sure, his awareness of the muscles and their requirements professional, positive. As was his voice, now so close to her ear, murmuring, rumbling, the words sometimes distinct, sometimes so soft that she could barely hear them.

Not that it mattered; what he was saying was only noise, nonsense, a soothing, repetitious rumble of sound such as one might use to calm a fractious animal. Or woman, she thought, just before she mumbled, 'I'm not a dog or a horse, you know.'

'I know,' he said, then lapsed again into the soothing of her tense muscles, his hands moving freely now along the contours of her back from waistline to shoulders, outlining the edges of her shoulderblades, playing piano down the nubbles of her spine, but now in silence—and suddenly that silence changed the entire atmosphere of the thing.

No longer was it simply a massage. Now his fingers were tracing the lines of her body, memorising them, reading the texture of her skin, the flow of the now relaxed muscles beneath the skin, the contours, the hollow of softness at the base of her spine, the flex of her ribs.

When she'd taken off the sweatshirt, the movement had loosened the band holding her hair in the crude ponytail; now she felt his hands completing the job, felt the caress as he freed her hair and spread it down across her neck and shoulders, sensed rather than felt him lifting a hank of it to his nostrils under the guise of arranging her mane to suit his purpose.

Sensed it? Perhaps imagined it, she thought, until his voice, softer now than before, murmured a single word.

'Beautiful.'

'What is?'

She was able to ask the question calmly, without the earlier tensions he had so effectively erased. She had never been actually afraid of him, only embarrassed by the situation, by the deliberately contrived circumstances. But no longer; with his touch had come assurance, relaxation. Just as he had intended.

'You...your hair...your skin...'

Now she did feel his mouth against her hair, and his words were a caress against the shell of her ear—a caress followed by another as his lips brushed against the skin relaxed by those sensitive fingers. His lips touched her ear, his fingers now moving down along her neck, touching at her shoulders and nape with a different touch, one that recognised his words, recognised their real meaning.

Colleen sighed, leaning back instinctively against his hands so that she could feel his chest against her back, could get closer to him, even more comfortable. Because now his touch had changed again; now it had the softness of his breath, the recognition of her as more than just a model—as a woman.

The tip of his tongue flicked at her earlobe before tracing fire down the nape of her neck. The tip of a finger slid its bumpy path down her spine before halting to circle images of delight around that sensitive soft spot at its base.

Colleen sighed; the sound echoed from lips that now nibbled at the lobe of her other ear, the breath of it stirring her hair, the sensation stirring her insides until she thought she might melt. His strong hands had closed about her waist; she was already stirring herself to help him as he moved to shift her round to face him. His fingers flexed, stroked, caressed, lifted...

And she was thumped back down on her tailbone, landing so hard her teeth clicked together.

'This isn't getting the sketching done, Ms Ferrar.'

And his voice was hoarse, almost menacing, though ragged with unquestionable emotion. Before she could speak he was up and moving back across the room, leaving her slumped with her head on her knee, no longer tense but trembling now, at least in the pit of her stomach, at the centre of her womanhood.

It was of little satisfaction to hear his voice audibly shaking a bit too, as he gruffly ordered her to lift her right arm a bit, turn her head slightly to the right, shift her rump here, her shoulders there...

The sound of his pencils briskly swishing across the sketch pad seemed to vibrate like a wind through the room, but the sensation of his touch was more of an echo, continuing to vibrate through her body, keeping her mind in a maelstrom of confusion as she mechanically obeyed his orders in silence, until with an explosive grunt of what seemed to be satisfaction he threw down pencil and paper and marched towards the door, not even so much as looking at her.

'I'm going to step out and visit the dog,' he said quietly over his shoulder. 'That'll give you the privacy to get something on, and then maybe you could make us a coffee and I'll give you a progress report on your father's *maybe* birthday present. OK?'

Colleen muttered her assent, then leapt to her feet once the door had closed and shrugged into her sweatshirt as quickly as if she'd been freezing, although it wasn't being cold that made her continue to tremble. It was the memory of his touch, the feel of his breath against her cheek…and her own uncertainty now about what it all meant.

Had it been, she wondered, a calculated move to disorient her, to impress upon her his ability to arouse with such consummate ease? Or had it, perhaps, unbelievably, surprised Devon Burns as much as it had her?

There might have been no handy pile of sawdust as he'd mentioned in the restaurant, but it hadn't been needed either! He could have taken her—there and then—and she would have helped him, welcomed it! Beyond all question he must have known that, perhaps had even deliberately arranged it so. But to what possible purpose?

She looked at the sketch pad, moved a step in that direction, then gave herself a mental shake and turned away towards the kitchen instead. She filled the kettle and turned it on, spooned instant coffee into cups, and gradually, deliberately, gave vent to the feelings of an-

ger that came from having been so obviously manipulated.

By the time Burns returned she was standing over the
coffee-table, sketch-book in hand, all feelings of anger
dissipated by the sheer artistry of what she was looking
at. There were broad general views, but most stirring
were detail sketches of such small specific areas—the
bend of an elbow, the wing-like curve of a shoulder-
blade, the fall of hair against a nubble of spine.

She looked up as he entered, half expecting to see
some sign of protest or objection, but he only raised
one eyebrow and smiled—a weary gesture that revealed
in an instant how much mental effort had been put into
the work she was seeing.

'What do you think?' he asked softly. 'Went well, I
think, once we finally got going.'

'I…I should say so,' was all Colleen could muster.
The sketches she'd looked at were beyond that description, far beyond it. 'You…you look exhausted, though.'

Burns glanced at his wrist-watch, then flexed his right
wrist obviously. And now his smile was wider. 'We
were at it for a fair while. I'm actually surprised you're
not just a bit stiff now too. You did marvellously, by
the way.'

'Thank you, I think,' she replied. 'Now come and sit
down and have your coffee before it cools.'

He slid into an armchair in what seemed to be one
single fluid movement, picked up his cup, sipped at the
coffee, put it back down again and leaned back in the
chair to look at her.

'I promised you a progress report,' he said. 'And I'm
sure you'll be pleased to know I should have no problems now getting the Huon pine piece I promised you
done in time for your father's birthday. Whether you'll

like it or not...' He shrugged, then grinned. 'Well, I like it anyway. So far.'

Colleen nodded, touched by the sudden awareness that their entire relationship had changed somehow, that the tenseness and friction of it was diminished, altered.

'You've been busy, then, since I...saw you last?'

'Enough.' Another shrug, this one enigmatic, almost dismissive. 'I've had a few other things to take care of as well, but...yes—enough.'

'And you're happy, I gather, with what you've done today.' Not really a question, although meant as one. She knew that he was happy with what he'd done; he'd already said so.

'You've looked at the sketches...what do you think?'

'I'm no judge, but they certainly looked splendid to me,' she said. 'I was surprised at the...detail you seem to need, but I suppose it's all part of the process.'

'Every little bit helps. I'll still need you to sit for me in the studio, but perhaps not for as long now.'

'And there's still the front to do,' she muttered, hardly aware that she was speaking aloud. It wasn't a complaint, merely an observation.

Devon's bark of laughter was like a thunderclap in the room. 'And the sides,' he said, eyes twinkling as he shook his head in genuine amusement. 'Don't forget the sides, whatever you do. Ah, Colleen, you've a rough trot ahead of you if being a model is all this traumatic.'

Colleen grinned back at him; it had struck her as funny too, knowing how her muttered comment must have sounded. Knowing too that she hadn't been complaining or worrying, merely...

'I was just thinking that it's easier for me to sit still than it is for you to draw,' she replied in the calmest voice possible. 'Now, have you got all you can handle for today, or do you want to go on?'

One dark eyebrow raised itself into a question—the obvious question. Then he set down his coffee-cup, the entire movement seemingly in slow motion, it was so deliberate. He nodded, but didn't speak.

'Right, then,' she said, wishing that she felt as calm as she sounded, praying that her knees wouldn't betray her as she got up and marched towards the sofa, pulling the sweatshirt over her head as she did so.

'Right,' he agreed, but when his eyes focused on her bared breasts the look was almost disappointingly professional. So was the voice which directed her into the positions he wanted.

As she lifted her arms to fling the hair back over her shoulder, Colleen did fancy that she noticed just a tiny bit of tremble in the pencil in his fingers. She was probably imagining it, she thought, and hoped that she wasn't.

CHAPTER SIX

COLLEEN'S voice echoed through the studio, seeming to scatter the dust motes that played in a shaft of sunlight from one of the many windows.

'It isn't fair. I've said it before and I still say it.'

'What isn't fair? That you should keep on trying to distract me, or that you should be so unsuccessful at it?' Devon Burns replied. His amber eyes laughed at her, his even white teeth sharing the joke. The rest of him, hidden behind the screen that masked his work from Colleen's view, probably did too, she thought.

One dark eyebrow lifted, a corner of that incredibly mobile mouth twisted in thought, and she heard the gentle hiss of his chisel as it pared off some infinitesimal shaving from the wood in front of him—wood she could not see and therefore, perversely, wanted more and more to see.

'There is no reason whatsoever why you have to be so secretive about all this,' she insisted. 'I just don't think it's fair that I've been posing for you for nearly a *month* now, and I never get to see what you're doing!'

'You'll see it when it's done.'

'I might not live that long,' she sulked. She looked down at her body, naked but for the bottom of her bikini, and gave an exaggerated shiver. 'It's cold in here. Isn't it about time for a tea-break? Or is all this just an excuse for you to practise carving goose-bumps?'

Burns laughed, but when his eyes roamed across her body, at first professionally but then with undisguised

103

masculine appreciation, pausing at her slender waist, lingering to caress her breasts, the effect was startling even after all this time. The quickening pucker of her nipples under his gaze was definitely not goose-bumps!

Colleen had come easily enough to accepting her model's role. After her initial self-consciousness when he'd first sketched her at her flat, she had now relaxed to the point where she actually enjoyed the experience. Usually. But not when he looked at her *that* way, with eyes that plucked at her nipples, that turned her tummy to mush, her legs to jelly.

The problem, she thought, was that he only looked; ever since the day she'd first bared herself to the waist for him to begin his sketches, Devon Burns had treated her with... 'Circumspection' was the only word for it. He didn't make an issue of it, but she *knew* that she had suddenly become untouchable, inviolable. It was now a case of look but don't touch, which was fine in its own way except that Burns had made almost an obsession of it!

'You'll survive,' he said. 'In fact I think you're actually thriving on being a model—or else it's just because you enjoy tempting and tormenting me every chance you get.'

'I do no such thing!' But she did, and Colleen knew in her heart of hearts that it was so. And more, she did it deliberately, enjoying the sensation of being able sometimes—if rarely—to change the expression in those amber eyes, to boot out the professional and see the naked lust of the man behind him.

But sometimes, perhaps most times, she didn't truly understand just who was tempting and tormenting whom! There were moments when she was certain— positive!—that Devon Burns was leading her gently down some invisible garden path, using the safety of the aura he had himself created to entice her into a false complacency, a trap that would one day snap shut without warning.

'How could I possibly tempt and torment *you*?' she asked, trying to instil in her voice a sense of innocence that had no fair place there. She knew all too well how she'd been doing it—although she wasn't quite so certain just why! She was enormously attracted to this self-confessed misogynist, but her feminine vanity was bruised by the ease with which he seemed to discount her sexuality whenever she modelled for him.

'I might as well be a sheep sitting here, for all the difference it makes,' she continued. 'And you know it too. When you're working you're oblivious to temptation, or would be if there was any—which there isn't.'

'Now you're being paranoid,' he growled, but didn't even bother to look up. His eyes were fixed on his work, and Colleen felt certain that he was only half involved in the conversation.

'*Me* paranoid?' she cried. 'You've got a nerve saying a thing like that when you've gone to all this effort to protect the secrecy of...of whatever it is you're doing! I mean, really! What do you think I'm going to do—contaminate your work just by looking at it?'

She looked round his enormous studio, where various pieces of work in progress were hidden beneath shrouds of burlap sacking as was the makeshift screen he had erected to ensure that she could not see anything of the sculpture for which she posed.

It was all quite ridiculous, she thought. Some of the pieces she had already *seen*; they hadn't been shrouded on her very first visit to the studio, but now he had gone into this annoyingly secretive mode, just to be difficult.

Now he paid attention. She looked over to see those amber eyes glaring at her.

'I told you right from the start that I'm superstitious about anybody seeing work in progress,' he growled. 'And you understood it then and you understand it now. The only difference is that your female curiosity is playing up and you just can't *stand* that, can you? Forbidden fruit, Colleen, and there are quite sufficient historical warnings about that. Not that I'd expect you to heed them, being as admittedly and undeniably female as you are, so it's up to me to protect you from yourself.'

And he grinned, the act transforming his face and denying the growl he had kept in his voice throughout.

'Oh…rubbish, rubbish, rhubarb, rhubarb,' she snapped. 'I'm surprised you'd admit to being *that* superstitious—a grown man like you. It's quite ridiculous.'

'It might be ridiculous, but it works for me,' he replied without hesitation. 'Why don't you just put it down to my artistic temperament and stop fussing about it?'

'Because it offends me, that's why,' she replied, knowing that she was being unreasonable, and also increasingly aware that she was becoming illogically cranky.

'Did you get out of the wrong side of the bed this morning?' he asked, but without raising his head this time, so that she couldn't actually *see* the gleam in his eyes which she knew just had to be there. 'Or was it, perhaps, the wrong bed entirely?'

'I beg your pardon?' she said, unable or unwilling to believe what she'd just heard. Was this Devon Burns, boy misogynist, questioning her about…? 'I think you've got a cheek,' she snapped, realising that yes, he was indeed. 'It's absolutely none of your business, for starters, and I'd like to know why you're asking such a question in the first place.'

'It seemed reasonable enough,' he said with a shrug. 'You've been extremely cranky ever since you got here, and I certainly haven't given you any reason to be that way.'

But he *was* the reason, and she wasn't about to admit that to him.

'And, in case you hadn't noticed, it doesn't quite fit in with the seductress role you seem to have decided is part of being a model. Either you should be cranky—or seductive. Not both and certainly not both at the same time. It's far too distracting, and frankly I'm getting a bit fed up with it.'

'You…you…' She couldn't get any further. Her mouth kept working but for some reason the words stayed jammed in behind her teeth, locked in by a growing sense of anger, frustration…and guilt. He was right about her playing the temptress role—but she couldn't admit that, and wouldn't!

During the five, no, she mused, *six*—counting today—times she had modelled for him, Colleen had almost thought that she and Devon Burns might actually become friends. They had discussed a broad variety of things, found some common ground and some areas of discussion best left alone, but overall it had been a quite pleasurable experience.

Except, of course, for his professionalism—the way he could spend hours looking at her and yet not looking at her, seeing her as a model but not as a woman, not as…well, whatever.

She'd been gratified by that attitude at first, especially during her debut performance as a half-naked model.

But once her self-consciousness had been overcome...
Damn him, she thought, he knew what the problem
was—knew it and was playing on it, and had been all
along. He'd ignored her vanity and deliberately used it
along with her curiosity against her.

'I haven't the faintest idea what you're on about,' she
insisted, but didn't even *dare* attempt to meet his eyes.

'Stop being obtuse, Colleen. You've been playing
around with this temptress role right from the start,' he
said, laying down his chisel and rising to stretch in a
movement that tightened the T-shirt across his muscular
chest.

He paused to adjust yet another burlap shroud carefully over the siren figure, casually brushed the sawdust
from his fingers on jeans that fitted like a second skin,
then stalked out from behind the screen and over to
where he could loom ominously above her, arms folded
across his chest, his entire presence dominant, masculine, almost menacing.

'*And* you've done it deliberately. *And* you know you
have,' he said with a glowering scowl as he prowled
her body with his eyes, flexing and unflexing his fingers
as if to keep himself from reaching down and grabbing
her. 'And, what's more, you've done it under the pro-
tection of my professional morality, which means
you've been taking unfair advantage...*very* unfair advantage.'

Again he prowled her body with his eyes, their expression both a caress and now, suddenly, a threat! His
grin was wolfish—Colleen couldn't be sure that he
wasn't putting on an act, and suddenly didn't dare even
to question it.

'And then you accuse *me* of being unfair. Well, it
isn't me who's flaunting myself, who's being so delib-

erately tantalising,' he said, drawling out the word, making a meal of it. 'Tantalising! Wonderful word, that. Sounds a good deal nicer than it *is*, my dear Ms Ferrar; you might think about that.'

Colleen started to reply, *wanted* to reply, but the words wouldn't come. They couldn't; he was right and they both knew it. What she didn't know was what price she now might face for having pushed him too far.

She almost laughed out loud at the thought. Price? That, surely, was a strange word for it, considering that she wanted nothing more than for him to drop his professional veneer and start seeing her as a woman, treating her as a woman. She watched him, calmly meeting his eyes and noticing the way his jaw muscles flexed as he ground his teeth in thought.

'I want you. You know that,' he said suddenly. 'I've wanted you from the beginning, from the first instant I saw you...delivered to me like a plump, tasty pigeon.' And the gesture of licking his lips was, she feared, only half in jest.

Colleen found herself cringing beneath his gaze; she felt powerless, without the will or ability to move. His eyes flickered across her, touching like a lash at every part of her body, as if aware of her arousal, then flashing up again to capture her eyes.

'But what is it *you* really want, Colleen?' he mused, not really asking *her* the question at all. 'A present for your father—some esoteric fancy involving those bits of wood with their sentimental value? Or is it, I wonder, something more devious but far less complicated than that...something I very likely shouldn't give you, but will anyway, I think, because I've had enough of your silly little female games—more than enough!'

A hand snaked out to capture her wrist, whipcord

muscles flexed as he lifted her to her feet. Amber eyes burned into her own, holding her as he gathered her in his arms, pulling her against him so that she could feel the heat of his body through the T-shirt.

'Maybe it's time we both found out what you want,' he whispered, his voice harshly soft, but not as harsh as the lips which swooped down to capture her mouth in a kiss that was savage, almost punishing. Colleen's lips were crushed in the assault, her mouth forced open to admit the explorations of his tongue, seared with the heat of his ragged breath, the fierceness of his passion.

At first she could hardly breathe, squeezed against his chest, her breasts flattened, her ribcage bound in iron. Then his grip relaxed, though not his kiss, and she felt the fingers of his other hand—those long, sensitive artisan's fingers, so delicate and yet so intensely *feeling* as they cupped her breasts, lifting each in turn, then encircled her tiny waist.

Colleen sighed, her back arched into the cup of his hands. She heard a moan of ecstasy, of pure delight. Hers? His? It didn't matter.

He lifted her then, as one might lift a child, holding her up above his head while he rained kisses on her breasts, her belly, her thighs. She gasped with pleasure. Gasped again as she was dropped back into cradling arms, as he turned away to the studio door, kicking it open and thrusting his way through it as he moved towards the house with her in his arms.

She was vaguely conscious of the big red dog lurching from his nap on the porch, raising a querulous moan that Devon Burns first ignored, then commanded to cease as they passed.

She was vaguely aware of being carried into the house, down a hall she didn't know, into an enormous bedroom she'd never before seen, of being gently deposited on the softness of the waiting bed, of fingers touching her shoulders, touching her everywhere, like tiny brands of lightning. Of lips that followed the touch of those fingers—lips that burned, that seared with cold fires, then warm ones.

She was beyond objection now. Her body burned, flaring to his every touch, to every kiss, every caress, every brush of his muscular torso. Colleen reached up to pull his head towards her, every fibre of her being crying out for more of his kisses, more of his lovemaking, more of…everything!

Her fingers tangled in the thick hair at his neck, feeling the massive muscles beneath, the warmth of them, the strength…

'Love me.' Was that her own voice? It rang in her ears, but she was hardly aware of its echo. Her only real awareness was of fingers making magic with her skin, lips that burned, that chilled.

'Love me!'

Definitely her own voice that time, as fluttery as the mob of butterflies in her tummy, the small furnace beneath them sending wave after wave of delicious heat through her entire body.

But then came the ice water that dampened the flames, turning it all to black, cold ashes.

'What's love got to do with anything?' a sinuous voice whispered in her ear. Ending the magic, ending…ending everything but the torment caused by the caressing fingers, the greedy heat of the body against her own.

She wanted to reply, but his lips now stopped her mouth, keeping her answer inside her forestalled by the passion he could create, that she couldn't resist and yet knew, somehow, that she must resist. Now.

'Stop.' The word emerged as the barest of whispers against the torment of his kiss, but it slowed him, gave him just enough pause for her to repeat it, louder this time.

Again his mouth stopped hers, his kiss demanding, insistent. His hands had never paused in their knowing exploration of her body, turning her skin to such a state of sensitivity that she could not suppress a moan of pleasure.

'Please.' She breathed the word against the welcome but unwelcome intrusion of his tongue, knowing that she was fighting not only Devon Burns now but her own treacherous body, so thoroughly sensitised to his touch that her mind seemed incapable of regaining control.

'Please what?'

'Please stop,' she insisted, but it was insistence only from her mind; her body was aflame, beyond all control but his. And he knew it.

'Stop what?' he replied. 'This? Or this? Or...this?' And his fingers—those damnably sensitive fingers— provoked answers that refuted her own vocal denials, turned her brain to mush, then stroked once again the fire beneath her fluttery tummy.

What was happening was everything she'd dreamed of, but also nothing; Burns's acid query about love had seen to that. Colleen, in a saner moment and with honesty, would have been the first to admit that she didn't know for certain just what love really was anyway, but *this*, she knew, definitely was not!

'Or this?' he whispered, the devil's voice in her ear, his fingertips still dancing over her skin.

Colleen couldn't reply, didn't get the chance before

his mouth moved to claim her kisses, then to slide in a blinding caress along the hollows of her throat before returning to taste her again.

And she clung to him; her mind objected but her body had its own rules, and her fingers revelled in the touch of his muscles, his smooth skin. Her mouth rejoiced at the taste of him even as she fought for the control to resist his lovemaking, or punishment...or whatever it was. Her arms were locked around his neck when he surged up from the bed, carrying her with him, again cradled in his arms.

His mouth held her lips. Colleen writhed, seeking the freedom she didn't really want, but his grip held as he reached his feet, turned, moved away from the threatening bed.

'It's a pity,' he murmured into her neck. Or she thought he did; the words were indistinct, their tone deceptive. She let go, leaned away to try and see him, perhaps to hear better, but it was too late—he was already dropping her!

The water in the hot tub had been allowed to cool; Devon Burns didn't use the gigantic redwood tank often enough to warrant keeping it heated. But to Colleen's fevered skin the water was icy as she plunged unwittingly into it—dropped from Burns's arms with totally accuracy so that she landed fair in the middle and was totally submerged.

Surprise had caused her to draw a huge, gasping breath even as she fell, but even so she emerged with a splutter both of rage and inhaled water. Emerged to find him not laughing, as she might reasonably have expected, but standing in the bedroom doorway, arms folded imperiously across his chest, almost a statue in his rigidness. His voice was equally rigid.

'That ought to cool you off a touch,' he said. 'I suppose I ought to apologise for all this, but I'm damned if I'm going to. I don't appreciate being messed about, Ms Ferrar; I don't appreciate your attempts to manipulate me, or your jolly little games of seduction. That kind of thing has been tried with me before—by experts; and I might say that you are no expert.'

Then he sighed, but it was a sigh of extreme exasperation, not of weariness. And his eyes remained hostile, bleak.

'I am a professional at my work,' he said then, and it was said not as a boast but as a simple statement of fact. 'And I had thought you were too, or I wouldn't even have begun this...arrangement. Business and... pleasure don't mix well in my world, and I'd have thought you'd have learned that lesson too, from what I've heard. Obviously I was wrong.'

Colleen started to interrupt, but he ignored her.

'You're a beautiful woman and I'd love nothing better than to make love to you, assuming the right time and place and willingness on both sides. But not until we've finished our business. This man-woman stuff is quite wonderful, in its place—but its place is *not* involved with my work!'

Whereupon he smiled, although Colleen fancied that it was more of a sneer than a smile, despite the even white teeth it revealed.

'And, just for the record,' he said, 'I'm just old-fashioned enough to want to make the running myself, if you don't mind. And just experienced enough to be suspicious any time a woman starts using her feminine wiles to get something without telling me what it is she really wants.'

Again she tried to interject, but was forestalled this

time by a dismissive wave of his hand. Colleen was so struck by his accusations that she had ceased to notice the relative coldness of the water, and beneath his icy gaze she had shrugged her way down under the surface so that only her head protruded.

It was ridiculous, she thought, to be huddled here in a not-so-hot hot tub while this unsufferable egoist harassed and lectured her not two minutes after he'd come within a whisker of making love to her. But no, she thought, not making love. Clearly to Devon Burns there was no love involved in this; had he finished what he'd begun, it would have been sex, but not love—not by anybody's standard.

No love, then, but a lecture still not complete.

'So if we're going to finish this project—and I assume you want *that* much,' he said, with that half-sneer still evident, 'then we will do so without any more of your little games and deceptions. I trust that is quite clear.

'Now I am going to give my honest dog a good long run, which should give you ample time to tidy up and get dressed. When I get back, the splendid pot-roast I've been preparing for our dinner should be ready, and I assume you might have settled down sufficiently to give it your total attention—which it deserves.'

He turned towards the door, half opened it, then turned back to face a still astonished, still silent Colleen.

'You might, I suppose, be just cranky enough to tell me where I can put my pot-roast, et cetera, et cetera, but since I also suppose you still do intend to keep to your side of this idiotic bargain, to the benefit of your father's birthday and my impending exhibitions, perhaps you could just put all that emotional stuff on hold—at least until after dinner.'

He was gone before she could reply, the door slamming behind him. Colleen couldn't even move, much less speak; she squatted in the tub, her soaked hair streaming down over her face and shoulders, totally flabbergasted by the intensity of his assaults but unsure whether it was the lovemaking or the lecture which had upset her the most.

It was bad enough to realise that she was quite hopelessly in love with a man who didn't even believe in the word, but to be accused of being no more than a manipulative schemer was adding insult to injury.

'And I suppose I'm just expected to accept all this like a good little girl—even ignore that bit about my not being any sort of expert in seduction,' she muttered as she combed back her hair with her fingers and prepared to clamber out of the tub. 'Well, have I got news for you, Mr High-and-mighty Devon Burns!'

Except for her hair, it was the work of moments to get dried off, and then Colleen was free to prowl the room, her still wet hair confined by an impromptu turban formed from the towel. A glance out of one window revealed Devon Burns far out in a paddock, throwing retrieving dummies for the big red dog and obviously intending to do just what he'd said he would.

The bedroom was almost spartan in furnishings; those there were, however, had quite probably been handmade and most had obviously been carved by Burns into the bargain. There was a double bed—so tightly made that even their earlier writhings had barely disturbed it—an enormous wardrobe, several bookcases and a chest of drawers that ranged right across one end of the large room. The hot tub and adjoining bathroom took up the other end.

Each piece of furniture was superb in itself; each

drew the eye and held it—to the point where it took a moment or two before Colleen realised that none of the pieces matched. The fact tweaked her curiosity, but not enough to give her much pause; a moment later she was standing in his kitchen, hands on hips, fiercely debating with herself whether to spike the pot-roast with liberal lashings of cayenne pepper before she dressed and left.

'What a good idea,' she muttered aloud, but with second thoughts she set it aside in favour of returning to the studio where her clothes awaited. It seemed ridiculous but she felt a sudden apprehension about still being half-naked should Burns return before she could escape the place.

She spared another quick glance up to the paddock as she crossed between studio and house. Yes, he was still working with the dog and now even further away, probably heading for the big dam where she had helped him train Rooster by throwing dummies on a previous visit. She entered the studio and quickly changed into her jeans and T-shirt, wishing for a moment that she'd had the sense to put on a bra before starting out. At the time it had seemed irrelevant—she was only going to take it off along with almost everything else—but now, surprisingly uncertain, made self-conscious by Burns's lecture, if not his lovemaking, she wished...

'It hardly matters if you're not going to stay for tea,' she rebuked herself. And staying was not, she determined, a part of her plan. Not any more. She didn't have to give up on the project, didn't have to welch on their agreement—she would uphold her end of the bargain as agreed. But not now, not today. 'Besides, I agreed to model, not to provide stimulating dinner conversation,' she said.

And she was turning to the door, handbag in her

hand, when the enormity of Burns's accusations struck her in a rekindled flurry of anger.

There, not fifteen feet away, was the carefully screened, burlap-shrouded figure that he had been so absolutely insistent she must not see. For reasons that made no sense whatsoever! And there, many hundreds of metres away, was the man himself, safely and handily out of the way along with his lectures and his silly superstitions.

Did she dare? 'Do I dare *not*?' she muttered, already moving towards Burns's improvised barrier, already more than half-committed.

An instant later she was poised, fingers hovering over the burlap shroud and fairly quivering with anticipation. Or was it fear? she thought, turning quickly to scamper over to the window, from where she could double-check on Burns's location. Reassured, she returned and plucked away the burlap before her courage failed entirely.

Then she could only stand there, shaking her head with bewilderment and total confusion. There was no black-heart sassafras figure there, no half-naked sea-witch siren with flowing hair and a face supposedly like her own.

Perched in the wood-carver's vice, grinning up at her with an evil, lolloping-tongued grin, was a nearly completed sculpture, in what she could now recognise as Tasmanian myrtle, of Devon Burns's damned dog!

It made no sense. Colleen looked round the studio, her eyes darting from one burlap-covered article to another and then back to the piece in front of her.

It isn't possible; he didn't have time...he couldn't have had time...it's...it's just...madness... The words and phrases rushed helter-skelter through her mind as she put the burlap back in place, carefully arranging it to be exactly as she'd found it.

And her mind was still whirling madly as she scampered again to the window, then returned to prowl the entire studio, lifting and replacing each individual covering on each individual piece of work in the place.

No siren. No human figure of any kind whatsoever! Even more confusing—no piece of work involving the Huon pine she'd brought him. Not a one. She couldn't believe it—refused to believe it. Ignoring now the marginal risk of getting caught out, she went through the room in a deliberate, systematic search, looking beneath benches, into what were obviously storage places, checking spaces that were laughably too small or obviously empty.

'It doesn't...make...sense,' she muttered over and over and over throughout her extensive and totally futile search. And it didn't! But it would, she determined, after looking out the window to see Burns and Rooster heading home again.

She was waiting, although certainly not patiently, when they entered the house yard. She even had her mouth open to start the war when she suddenly realised that she couldn't!

CHAPTER SEVEN

THE realisation struck her like a hammer blow just as Burns and the dog rounded the corner of the house, and Colleen could only stand there, her mind in shredded disarray, and watch as they approached.

She couldn't—didn't dare—launch into the scathing attack she had planned, demanding from Burns an explanation about how he could justify having her pose half-naked for a sculpture of a dog. How could she? It would be a tacit admission that she was guilty of exactly what he had accused her of—snooping and deception.

Although, she thought, *he* had a cheek even to mention deception, given what he'd been up to. Having her pose like that—not once but several times—and now she didn't even know if he'd *ever* actually used her posing for the siren sculpture she had seen only when it was partially completed.

The whole thing made no sense whatsoever; any way she looked at it, Devon Burns had been leading her down some garden path or another right from the start, and Colleen wished for an instant that she *had* spiked his pot roast—with arsenic. But of course she hadn't—nor could she.

But neither could she obey her earlier instinct just to get dressed and get out before his return; it was far, far too late for that.

And, what was worse, Burns somehow *knew*. There was that look in his eyes again—the one that told Colleen he knew, either of her predicament or her deception or both. A look that also told her he was certain of his ability to be in control, to maintain that control. Because she was in love with him, and she very much feared that he knew that too, and that he wasn't above using the knowledge as it suited him.

Well, he wouldn't, she decided. He wouldn't be allowed to because she wouldn't let him, although just how she was going to achieve that bit of magic she wasn't at all sure. But as she stood there, arms folded across her bosom in a half-conscious gesture of defiance which Burns appeared to ignore, Colleen began to lose her feeling of uncertainty.

She wasn't some teenager, a victim of a calf-love crush on a screen idol. She was a woman grown, and even if she wasn't—as Burns had indeed suggested— any expert at seduction, she was certainly old enough and experienced enough to keep this insufferable egotist from winning every hand, from taking every trick. There *was* an explanation for all this; there simply had to be. And she would have that explanation or know the reason why!

How dare you accuse *me* of being deceitful? she thought, and realised almost too late that if she kept up that repetitive train of thought those would be the first words out of her mouth.

Rooster solved that problem. Sighting Colleen, he gave a throaty yodel of greeting and flung himself forward, rearing up to place his forepaws on her shoulders and slaver over her with wet, sloppy kisses as he almost knocked her over in his exuberance.

Burns's angry command was ignored. Colleen found herself hugging a damp, muddy, boisterous dog that seemed absolutely determined to drown her in affection.

'You great oaf. Get down! Down, you fool,' she

cried, finally managing to push the big Chesapeake away. 'Sit!' she demanded then, one forefinger poised in admonishment. And to her great surprise he did.

'I may shoot you, dog,' Burns said as he strode forward to grasp Rooster by the scruff of his neck, glaring down at him, amber eyes meeting amber eyes in a brief contest of wills. It was no contest; Rooster quickly glanced away and tried to roll over in submission, his own eyes turning to Colleen as if for moral support.

'Bloody great fool of a dog,' Burns muttered, rising with unexpected suddenness to stand looking down at Colleen, his eyes taking in the mud that was smeared all down the front of her. His own trousers were muddy—an unavoidable hazard of retriever-training in water—but Colleen looked as if she'd been swept with a dirty broom.

'Are you all right?' The question somehow seemed to hold more than politeness. Burns's manner at least seemed to show a measure of genuine concern.

'Of course. He was just being friendly.' Colleen looked down at her muddy clothes. 'Although perhaps a bit too friendly.'

Whereupon her irreverent mind leapt to her mouth. 'It looks as if that bath you forced on me might have been just a bit premature.'

'That's one way to describe it, I guess,' Burns replied, his eyes suddenly unreadable. 'He knows better too, or at least he should. I don't know what it is about you, but do me a favour and please don't ever turn up at a retrieving trial without me knowing it; I'd be a laughing stock if he pulled a stunt like that when he was supposed to be working, and I'd have the devil's own time controlling the great horror with you around.'

'Wouldn't you just,' she replied, her mind flashing to

the kennel-control magazine she'd noticed on an earlier visit. It would serve him quite right too, she thought, lodging the idea firmly at the back of her mind and wondering how she could sneak another look at the magazine without him catching her at it. All the trials would be listed, surely, and...?

'Which is a pity,' he was saying. 'There's a trial next weekend, and I *had* been planning to ask if you'd like to come, but after that little performance, and now, seeing the mischief in your eyes... Really, Colleen, you shouldn't even *try* to scheme like that.'

'Like what?' she demanded, forcing a tone of incredulity into her voice even while she knew that it wasn't likely to deceive Devon Burns. Bad enough that he could read her like a book without him having to prove it at every opportunity!

'You know very well *what*,' he replied. 'And so do I, because you're as transparent as glass. Everything you're thinking just comes out in your eyes like they were great, huge billboards.'

'I do *not* know,' she insisted. 'Not that it matters anyway. How could you even *think* I'd go anywhere with you after what you...well...you know?'

'I do? Well, I suppose I do, if you're referring to your little dunking. And I assume you are. I also assume you're waiting for an apology, but I told you then and I tell you now that you won't get one. You've been playing games with me, and you know it and I know it, and you got no more than you deserved. Probably less, in fact, because I have a strong suspicion there've been transgressions I don't even know about yet.'

Too accurate, too perceptive. Especially when he kept looking at her like that. Even if she had been able to create a suitable riposte, Burns's uncanny ability to stay just one step ahead of her was disconcerting, unnerving. Did he somehow know about her little snooping expedition? Had he arranged it even? It wouldn't have surprised her, but she was damned if she was going to admit it without him bringing up the subject first. It wouldn't be so bad, she thought, if he wasn't always so insufferably sure of himself!

Like now.

'I'd be happy to lend you something to change into if you like; unless you fancy eating dinner looking like that,' he said as he held open the door for her with one hand and waved the big red dog back with the other. And before Colleen could reply he added, 'Of course you *could* wear your modelling clothes, if you'd prefer. I'd even run you another bath.'

Colleen had to struggle to keep from belting him right there and then. After all his hoo-ha about her tormenting him, leading him on, after raging at her and lecturing at her and throwing her into his cold hot tub...*now* he wanted to make seductive suggestions himself?

She almost screamed, then replied as calmly as she could, 'I'm quite comfortable like this, thank you.'

But Colleen's most scathing glare went begging; Burns only laughed, showing his delight at having got her goat yet again. He then added insult to injury by licking his finger and reaching out to brush it across the line of her cheekbone, wiping away some real or imagined smudge. And when she flashed her own hand upwards in defence he only laughed the louder, reaching out to capture it with his other hand while he completed the job.

'Might as well have the boy in while we're at it, then,' he said with a chuckle. 'I reckon he's no grottier than you.'

'He's probably got better table manners too,' Colleen snapped, struggling vainly to free her hand. 'Maybe you could send us both to the kennels so that you can dine in proper style.' And she looked pointedly at his own muddy trousers, then looked away again without saying another word.

Burns, damn his eyes, she thought, didn't even have the decency to grant her the point.

'I simply didn't want you to feel at a disadvantage when you're savouring the delights of my culinary skills,' he said, still not releasing her hand. 'I am one of the world's truly great pot-roasters, I'll have you know. People have come from all over the world just to *smell* one of my pot-roasts.'

'And to be overwhelmed by your modesty as well, I'm sure,' Colleen replied, no longer so sure that even now she shouldn't spike the dinner with cayenne pepper. The thought was deliciously tempting until she realised she too would have to suffer the consequences.

'That also,' he said with a grin, finally releasing her hand, but not before giving it a thorough inspection, looking first at her palm, then turning the hand over, almost but not quite as if he planned to kiss it. 'Now come and get scrubbed up; you've a treat ahead of you, I promise.'

His attitude was infectious, and by the time they'd 'scrubbed up' Colleen was finding it increasingly difficult to maintain even a semblance of her earlier chagrin. It would all be much, much easier, she decided, if only Devon Burns had the same consistent temperament of his big red dog, instead of being so mercurial that she never knew what to expect.

She followed him towards the kitchen, her mind still awhirl with questions that she wanted to ask but didn't dare—at least not directly. What had happened to the siren sculpture? And even more important—what had he been up to, having her pose for it when it wasn't there? It seemed ludicrous for him to have kept her posing for a carving of Rooster; in fact it made no sense at all. And what about the Huon pine, the sculpture he'd promised for her father's birthday? Surely he had no reason to hide that?

The feeling of confusion was strong, but even stronger was the feeling that somehow, quite deliberately, she was being set up! The problem for Colleen was that she didn't know why, couldn't imagine exactly how, and had no idea what she could, or should, do about it.

'You'll fall in love with this,' he was saying as he lifted the pot lid in a flamboyant gesture, leaning over to sniff appreciatively at the contents. He motioned to Colleen to join him, and she was about to do so, if grudgingly, when a roar of barking erupted outside, followed by a distinctly feminine cry of alarm.

'Don't tell me that damned dog has brought me another pigeon,' Burns said, clapping the lid back on his pot-roast before he dashed to the front door with Colleen not far behind. Neither of them, she suspected, was quite prepared for what they saw, and Colleen was certainly unprepared for Devon's reaction to it.

'Rooster—*get out of it*!' he shouted, and rushed forward to grab at the red dog's collar. Rooster, growling fiercely, was doing his best to wrest a closed umbrella from the hands of a tall, elegantly dressed blonde woman who was backed up against her car, shrieking at the dog in some foreign language. The words were quite unintelligible but it didn't take much imagination to guess at their meaning. Either way, Rooster was decidedly unimpressed; Colleen was certain that his growls were ominously different from his normal vocabulary.

'*Out of it*!' Devon roared, and finally the dog condescended to listen, although not without shooting his master a scathing glare as he relinquished the umbrella and stalked haughtily away to stare at the scene from a distance.

'Devon...darling; thank God you're here!' cried the blonde, dropping the umbrella and inching forward in her fashionably tight skirt to take Devon's hands in her own. 'I was afraid that awful creature was going to eat me.' Her grey eyes were alight with the excitement, and her carefully arranged hair had been shaken from its perfect *coiffure*.

'You should have known better than to try and hit him with that thing, Ingrid. I'm surprised he didn't take your arm off,' Burns replied, holding the woman's hands and drawing her closer to him. Or was it she doing the drawing close? Colleen wondered. But there was no question at all about who instigated the kiss that followed.

'I did not strike the dog,' the blonde insisted after she had released his mouth. 'I was merely concerned about him leaping all over me; that is obvious, is it not?'

'Perfectly,' Burns replied. And his eyes roamed with all too obvious appreciation over her tall, slender, truly elegant figure—figure, Colleen couldn't help but notice with a professional eye, that was garbed in a very chic, very flattering wool suit that fairly screamed expensive and exclusivity. As it should, she thought, although perhaps not *quite* so loudly; it was a copy of one of her own better designs, not an original—a survivor of her war with Andrew.

'But it would take more than that dog, Ingrid, to disrupt your style,' said Burns.

'Always you are the flatterer,' was the smiling reply, but Colleen noticed that there was no smile in those cool grey eyes when the woman glanced over to where Rooster still bristled. There was naked dislike in that glance, and Colleen sensed that the feeling was mutual; Rooster was not impressed with this pigeon. And there was neither a smile nor any semblance of warmth when the woman noticed, seemingly for the first time, Colleen standing in the open doorway.

Those grey eyes flickered over Colleen with a haughty insolence that quickly turned to contemptuous dismissal as they took in her mud-smeared clothing and disarranged hair, instantly categorising her as irrelevant—although perhaps with some reservations. It was a look which she was all too familiar with, and Colleen had to smile inside at how much the haute-couture attitude was out of place in this rural setting.

Having categorised and dismissed Colleen, the blonde woman returned her attention totally to Devon, whose hands she still held in a gesture that bespoke long familiarity.

'Ah, Devon…it is so good to finally get here,' she said in a voice like cut silk. 'I have been flying non-stop, virtually, from Paris, darling,' the woman continued. 'And I am quite totally exhausted. All that I want is perhaps one hour in your wonderful spa, yes? And then twenty-four hours, at least, of sleep.'

'Well, the spa wants heating up; it hasn't had much use lately. You'd best have dinner with us first,' was the reply. And Colleen wasn't quite sure that he didn't flash a quick, cryptic glance in her direction as he mentioned the spa.

'And your timing is just about perfect too, Ingrid; Colleen and I were just about to sit down.'

Now the blonde woman did look at Colleen, and her earlier dismissal got a revaluing as Devon went through the formalities of an introduction.

Ingrid, whose surname turned out to be Johnsson, was Devon Burns's principal agent in Europe, and had come, he said, 'to hound and badger and harass me into getting my next exhibition ready quicker than I want to.'

Somewhat to Colleen's surprise, he adroitly avoided providing the blonde with any comparable details; he merely introduced Colleen by her first name and hustled them into the house, with Rooster following closely at their heels.

She probably thinks I'm the kennel maid or something, Colleen thought, not particularly concerned at the prospect somehow, then had to mentally shrug off the thought that perhaps Devon had deliberately tried to spare his agent any possible embarrassment over meeting the designer of her not quite original outfit. Burns was, Colleen was certain, quite capable of knowing that much about women's fashion. He might even have bought Ingrid the suit, she thought uncharitably, and flinched inwardly at her own cattiness.

She told herself that this was one of those times when anonymity had its merits. Then she told herself that she wasn't one whit perturbed by Ingrid's too deliberate attitude of possessiveness concerning Devon Burns. Then she decided that she might be better off out of this.

'You two will want to discuss business, I'm sure,' she said, even as Burns was steering them towards the dining room. 'Perhaps I'd best go and let you get on with it; I'm not especially hungry anywa—'

'You'll stay and sing the praises of this pot-roast or you'll find yourself fair at the top of my blacklist,' Burns growled, and his fingers clenched on her upper arm to reinforce the demand. Behind him, Ingrid's expression made it clear that she much preferred Colleen's idea.

'No, really, I don't want to intrude,' she replied, but her heart wasn't in it and she felt that they both knew it. What she didn't say was that it had already occurred to her that if he was going to show his work to Ingrid—as surely he must!—she too might have her curiosity satisfied.

Burns seated both women, then disappeared into the kitchen, returning a few moments later with an opened bottle of red wine and glasses for all of them.

'You lot can make a start on this,' he said. 'I'm just going to bring in your bags, Ingrid, and put a fire under that hot tub; you wouldn't fancy hopping in there the temperature it's at now.' With which he shot a gleeful smirk in Colleen's direction and walked out.

Rooster followed him, although not, Colleen noticed, without what she chose to interpret as a suspicious glare at the blonde Ingrid.

The feeling was obviously mutual; Ingrid gave a mighty sigh as the dog left the room and reached out one perfectly manicured hand to lift the wine bottle.

'I do hope Devon leaves that monster outside this time,' she confided as she filled the three glasses and passed one over to Colleen, glancing meaningfully at Colleen's mud-stained clothing as she did so. 'You also, I guess; that dog is a menace. Every time I am coming here he destroys something—the first time a pair of gloves, the last time a shoe. He has ruined several good pairs of stockings…always he is jumping up on me, the ill-mannered beast.'

Colleen looked ruefully down at her own clothing, thinking that it was messed up, fair enough, but hardly ruined. 'He's only a baby really,' she replied, then laughed inside at the strangeness of hearing herself parroting Devon's words, remembering that she hadn't been amused at hearing them when she'd first met Rooster. But as she listened to Ingrid's lengthy recital of the red dog's sins she realised that not only did the blonde not like Rooster, she was terrified of him. And, Colleen thought, very likely terrified of all dogs.

'You…are employed by Devon?' she was asked then, in an abrupt change of subject that caught her rather by surprise.

'No. I'm…well… I'm just sort of helping him out,' she finally replied, not wanting to be too specific without really knowing why. Ingrid's question hadn't seemed to be especially prying, but something about the blonde made Colleen instinctively cautious.

'Ah.' Again those bleak grey eyes assessed Colleen, then again appeared to dismiss her as irrelevant. Clearly this elegant, worldly woman didn't see competition in a mud-smeared nonentity. Her air of possessiveness— or was it simply extreme confidence and self-assuredness?—was total, all-encompassing. Now she demonstrated her familiarity with Devon and his world by first refilling Colleen's wineglass, then briskly laying out the cutlery and silverware to prepare for their host's return.

If the gesture was deliberate, it had the desired effect; in all her visits Colleen had never assumed nor been offered such familiarity. She had shared impromptu meals with Devon, had had coffee with him, but always with the strict sense that it was *his* home, totally under *his* control. Ingrid treated the place almost as if it were her own, even though from her remarks it seemed that she was at best an infrequent visitor.

Perhaps, Colleen thought, 'visitor' wasn't the appropriate word; Devon Burns and this cool, sophisticated blonde quite obviously had a very close relationship if she could drop in without notice or warning and feel assured of a hot tub and a bed—probably with Devon Burns in it. She thought for an instant of her own introduction to the huge redwood tub, then decided that it was better not to.

Colleen gave herself a severe mental shake; none of this was any of her business, and she was only punishing herself by speculating. Burns had never given her any encouragement to become emotionally involved; if he could have seen the green-eyed monster that was so casually destroying her appetite just now he would have laughed himself silly.

He seemed to be taking an inordinate amount of time to cope with the minor tasks he'd mentioned, she was thinking, when the door opened and Burns, laden with suitcases, trudged past—*en route*, Colleen assumed, to the bedroom.

'The amount of travelling you do, Ingrid, I'm surprised you haven't made yourself broke with overweight-baggage charges,' he said upon his return. 'Honestly, haven't you ever heard of the concept of travelling light?'

'But of course,' was the reply. 'This is what I am doing.'

He slid into a chair at the head of the table and sipped appreciatively at his wine before chuckling with wry amusement, 'If you say so; I only hope you tip well.'

'I…know how to express my appreciation,' she said, in tones that made it abundantly clear what she meant. Thankfully she stopped short of being any more specific, Colleen thought, but Devon didn't even seem to notice the innuendo.

Instead, he turned his attention to Colleen and asked if she, too, travelled the world with enough baggage to support a small army.

'Only myself,' she had to reply. 'Not that I've done that much travel overseas.'

'I've done my share, and expect I will again, but I still reckon the best part of any trip is getting home again when it's over,' he said surprisingly. She had never before discussed this with him, had not realised that he was so committed to his lifestyle and sense of roots. 'I haven't yet seen anywhere I'd rather live than here, when all's said and done.'

That comment was the springboard for a spirited and obviously long-standing argument between him and Ingrid about where he should be living. Ingrid apparently was convinced that he would be equally happy in Europe or even America; she made it all too clear that she thought Tasmania far too remote in the extreme, and, without saying so in just so many words, that having him accessible to *her* was the major criterion in her thinking.

'Bull-dust,' was his firm, almost disdainful response. 'I can be on a flight to almost anywhere in the world from here within a couple of hours if I plan it right. Assuming, of course, that I wanted to go in the first place. But try that some time from some of the places you'd have me based and you'd be hard put to get out of the suburbs in that time.' The argument slowed only long enough for him to serve the dinner, then re-

sumed with a vengeance as they dined. Colleen found
it fascinating, if occasionally too convoluted for her to
follow with any ease. Her own travel experience seemed
minuscule compared with that of these two, and she
found herself wondering when Devon had ever found
the time to make his international reputation.

Ingrid, for her part, seemed to be on the move so
much that she didn't apparently have a home as such,
and Colleen couldn't help but wonder how the blonde
Scandinavian could expect to maintain such a hectic
pace *and* the relationship she so obviously wanted with
Devon Burns at the same time.

But most surprising was the way Devon seemed to
ignore that element of Ingrid's thinking. He seemed,
from Colleen's viewpoint, to be quite unaware of the
blonde sophisticate's personal—as opposed to business—interest in him. He treated her as an old and valued friend, Colleen thought, but Ingrid's interest was
much more involved than that, even if he was apparently unaware of it.

Unaware? Or was it more a case of deliberate blind-
ness? she wondered. To her eyes, Ingrid's infatuation
was glaringly obvious, almost embarrassingly so. How
could Devon *not* see it? He was, she would have
thought, far too sensitive to be blind to Ingrid's feelings
except by choice.

Somehow, during Colleen's introspection, the subject
changed yet again; she returned to the present to find
Devon and Ingrid locked in dispute over something involving commissions, and his emphatic remark sounded
all too familiar in Colleen's ears.

'I don't *do* commissions,' he was saying. 'I do not
and will not and that's that, Ingrid. You know damned

well that I've been there, done that and will...not...
do...it...again!'

'You are still upset by that one incident? But that
was—what?—six, seven years ago now.'

Ingrid's surprise seemed genuine enough, if not quite
so emphatic as Devon's conviction.

'Not just that one incident—which, incidentally, has
finally been resolved, after a fashion,' he replied. 'But
I will admit, with hindsight, that it was quite enough by
itself to put me off commissions for ever; I just cannot
and will not have anybody else's opinion governing my
work like that. It's fine if they want to criticise a piece
once it's finished, but while it's in progress, damn it,
my work is mine and mine alone!'

'That *one* incident has made you into the world's
worst misogynist,' the blonde woman replied, making
no attempt—at least to Colleen's ears—to hide the bitterness in the remark. 'And, if you wish my professional
opinion, it has cut you off from an entire genre of work
that could have given international recognition far beyond what you already have.'

'I have all the recognition I need,' he said, but it was
another, younger Devon Burns talking now—a man hurt
and still suffering that pain. It was there in his voice,
in his eyes; he even went so far as to shake his head,
as if to try and dislodge the hurt...or the memory.

The resultant silence gave Colleen the opportunity
she had subconsciously been waiting for. This conversation was getting far too personal for her taste; there
were strong emotions here which she didn't feel up to
coping with, not to mention undercurrents that she
didn't understand and wasn't sure she wanted to.

'I think maybe it's time I shot through,' she said, the

words plopping into the silence with what seemed a
startling volume.

'No way! We're just getting to the interesting part,'
was the astonishing reply from her host. 'No, you stay,
Colleen. I'm about to show Ingrid the stuff I've assem-
bled for her next exhibition, and I'm sure you'll be interested in at least some of it.'

The remark brought an expression of curious concern
to the blonde Ingrid's ice-grey eyes; she looked at Colleen with the most astonishing mix of apprehension and
hostility—unlike Devon, whose eyes twinkled mischievously.

'All right.' What else could she say? If only, Colleen
thought, she didn't have that sinking feeling that Devon
Burns was deliberately manipulating her, and using her
own well-developed curiosity to do it!

'Right,' he said then with a vigorous grin, absolutely
leaping from the chair. 'Charge your glasses first, and
let's get on with it, then.'

Moments later the three of them, Rooster prowling
like a shadow behind them, were in Devon's studio,
blinking as their eyes adjusted to the glare of the fluo-
rescent lights. Devon dragged over a couple of alumin-
ium lawn chairs and waved the women into them.

And then, one by one and with a great display of
quite outrageously extravagant showmanship, he pro-
duced the various pieces he'd selected for Ingrid's exhibition—which Colleen now knew to be the one he'd
referred to as being nearly three months away, just before her father's birthday.

She watched, fascinated, as piece after piece was
brought out for display, duly commented upon, appropriately admired by both her and Ingrid, then returned
to its place in storage. Ingrid, while appreciative and

admiring of all the work, also seemed extremely perceptive in her comments from what Colleen realised was a highly developed professional point of view.

For herself, it was difficult enough just to keep her attention on what was going on. She had seen, however briefly, all of these pieces during her snooping earlier in the day, and while there was much to be admired her eyes kept straying to where she knew the siren sculpture should be—and wasn't.

How was Devon going to handle this situation? she wondered. He must either not show that piece to them at all, or...? Whatever, she was more than half-certain that he was aware of her divided attention, and also the reasons for it.

Her speculation ceased when he was about to bring out the next piece, commenting as he did so that Ingrid should find it especially interesting in view of their discussion about commissioned work. Colleen didn't pay that much attention at first, expecting that she had already seen it. But when he brought the piece from the storage cabinet she realised immediately that she had never seen it before.

To have seen this masterpiece and not remember would have been impossible—even Ingrid allowed herself a small hiss of genuine appreciation, while Colleen forcibly had to hold back a cry of wonder and delight—but that she should have missed it during her snooping expedition seemed even more impossible. It simply couldn't have happened, she thought.

'This might turn out to be the highlight of the exhibition if I decide to let you take it, Ingrid,' Devon said, without any trace of false modesty. 'I'm not sure if I'm prepared to sell it, and if I'm not there isn't much sense

you carting it all the way to Europe just to send it back
again.'

'I would do so gladly,' was the soft reply as Ingrid
rose from her chair and stalked round the figure that
Devon had placed on the display platform. 'But I will
not; this is too…too strong…it would overshadow everything else and then everyone would be wishing to
buy only this piece.'

Her excitement about the piece was revealed by the
slight thickening of her accent, and Colleen felt that she
knew exactly how Ingrid must be feeling. The work was
certainly strong; indeed, 'powerful' might have been a
better word for it. In some reddish wood—not myrtle,
she was certain—Devon had somehow blended animal
and human elements into a composite that might have
stepped alive from a woodland fantasy—or a nightmare.

At first glance the almost life-size figure was a were-
wolf, caught midway through its shape-change. A more
studied inspection revealed it to be a were*fox*, but that
was the least of its surprises. The figure was subtly and
yet undeniably sensual, erotic—whether animal or human or whatever between this was a vixen on heat.

The workmanship was what she might have expected
from Devon Burns, only more so—Colleen thought that
this might be the best thing he'd ever done. It had an
elemental simplicity, a primeval strength about it that
was both startling and yet exquisite. And explicit! Burns
had somehow managed to capture the essence of his
subject, and it was this essence of feralness, almost of
malevolence, which gave the statue its power. And its
face was familiar—surprisingly, almost frighteningly
so; it was a face that Colleen had seen only once but
had never been quite able to forget.

'I've called this a lot of other things since I did it,'

Devon said, with a harsh, almost sadistic grin. 'But I keep coming back to my first choice—*Vixen*—and may the foxes of the world forgive me.'

'Has that one?' Ingrid asked. 'From what you told me about this at the time I would have thought—'

'Not likely,' he interrupted. 'She hates me as much as she ever did—maybe a bit more. To be as fair as I can be, she's as spinny as a wheel, of course. Quite mad, although probably harmless to anybody but me. She still has this amazing fantasy that I fathered that poor bloody child, and I guess she'll hate me for ever just for that!

'But her husband has forgiven me, at last. He finally—after all these years—caught her out in her lying and craziness. And, to give the devil his due, he actually apologised and even returned this...along with a quitclaim—God only knows how he got her to sign that, and I don't think I even want to know—allowing its exhibition and sale at my discretion.'

Burns shrugged. 'He said it was partial compensation for keeping the piece from being exhibited for so long, but it isn't really. It was realising that child was his, after all that did it, I suspect. Still,' he said with a shrug, 'although in those days I could have used the exposure this is still one of the best things I've ever done. Maybe even *the* best.'

Again the shrug, but there was no complacency about it. It was an acceptance, if only a grudging acceptance.

'But, really, I was so damned glad to see he hadn't destroyed it—he threatened to at one point, as you know, Ingrid—that I didn't bother to discuss it with him.'

Burns turned to look at the statue, and Colleen could have sworn that his amber eyes actually *glowed* with the intensity of his emotions. The muscles of his strong jaw testified to the grinding of his teeth, and that lean, rakish body almost vibrated with tension.

'And if anybody's going to destroy the damned thing it'll be me!' he growled, then turned unexpectedly towards Colleen.

'What do *you* reckon?' he asked, his voice still raspy with the tension inside him. 'A decent likeness—both physically and…of what she is, the essence of her? Or do you even remember?'

'Oh, yes,' she replied, almost shrinking from the intensity of his inner anger, his pain. 'I remember—at least enough to vouch for the likeness. I don't know about the rest, except that she certainly *seemed* to dislike you very much.'

His short bark of laughter was sharp, as fiery as his eyes.

'Dislike? That's putting it mildly. That woman hates me even worse than she hates *that*,' he said, pointing to the sculpture. 'Because I'm *not* the father of her child and damned well couldn't be, and probably because that only *starts* to show her true character. I know exactly what she's like, the poor bitch—madness or no—and, for that, she could never forgive me. Whoever said that hell hath no fury like a woman scorned knew exactly what he was talking about. And so do I!'

He laughed then, but it was laughter fraught with bitterness and long-nurtured anger at the unfairness of it all.

'All this trauma—because of *that*?' Colleen was talking more to herself than to Burns, but he took the question literally.

'That's the crux of it, but it's a long and rather sordid little tale; I might tell you some time, if you catch me in a foul enough mood. But not tonight! Tonight we're looking to the future, not the past.'

And, having dismissed the subject, leaving more questions than answers in Colleen's mind, he set *Vixen* aside and turned his attention once more to the display of his work for the exhibition ahead.

He trotted out another half-dozen pieces of his work, each—like the first lot—unique and beautiful in its way. But in comparison with *Vixen* not one of them stood out. They were all dimmed in contrast to that splendid effort, and Devon Burns must have realised it.

'Of course, I have another potential focal point for the exhibition,' he said, this time with his attention focused more on Colleen than Ingrid. 'It's got the same intrinsic problem in that I'm not at all sure I want to sell it, but I'll let you two be the first to judge.'

With only that for an introduction he threw Colleen an enigmatic glance and walked over to gather in his arms the shrouded figure from behind the screen. The shroud was still in place as he reached the dais, but there was no shroud on the gleam of anticipation in his eyes as he grinned mischievously at Colleen and then removed it, leaving her to gasp in sheer astonishment.

CHAPTER EIGHT

INGRID, too, gasped with astonishment; Colleen felt the gesture from the blonde woman beside her. But whereas Ingrid's reaction was simply one of pure delight at the splendid creation being exhibited her own was far more complicated.

She half rose from her seat, panic flooding through her in an unleashed reaction to what she was seeing and what she had expected to see, but now didn't. What had happened? What strange magic trick had Devon Burns played this time?

The sculpture before them was not, as Colleen had quite confidently expected, the nearly completed depiction of Rooster. This was the black-heart sassafras siren in all its glory, completed, finished, polished...and absolutely magnificent!

Just as *Vixen* had exuded an aura of feral malignancy this siren sculpture had its own unique aura, but it was somehow one of purity and brightness. It was seductive, sensual, indeed erotic in every clean, sculpted line, but there was none of the taint that *Vixen* carried. The man seduced by the venality of *Vixen* was doomed, but *Siren* held only promises of wonder and beauty in its seductiveness.

And, of course, it had her face. Her face and... Colleen could almost feel herself blushing at the naked voluptuousness of the figure that posed on its spraywashed rock, hair like seaweed in the spume. Her figure? Surely not, she thought, but had to wonder.

And wondered even more at how Devon Burns had managed the miraculous transformation from what she had seen under this shroud only hours before to *this*! Only he could have done it, but she couldn't think when, much less how. Was she going quite mad?

The triumphant look in those damned amber eyes didn't help her. She couldn't tell if the triumph related to having caught her out yet again or was there simply because he was proud—and justly so—of the achievement she was now seeing.

Burns—wisely—was saying nothing. The work spoke for itself; indeed it fairly *sang*, in appropriate siren fashion, its song echoing the clarity and purity of the artistry, the sheer magic of it. The black heart of the sassafras—due, Colleen now knew, to a fungus within the structure of the wood itself—had been cunningly used to fullest advantage, giving highlights to the wind-washed hair, to the perch on which the siren poised.

But…*her* face? For an instant she knew exactly how the model for *Vixen* might have felt, even discounting the wickedness of character that piece revealed. It was disconcerting, almost frightening, the humanity Burns managed to instil into a piece of wood, how much the sculpture revealed, implied, suggested…

Colleen closed her eyes for a moment, as if that simple gesture could change anything. But when she opened them again the sculpture still sang, and now she could feel Devon Burns's eyes upon her, asking for a reaction, demanding a reaction. And, beside her, the cool grey eyes of Ingrid Johnsson, flickering from Colleen to the siren to Devon, then making the circuit again.

'Ah-h-h…' Ingrid's whisper said everything and yet nothing; Colleen had no way to judge if the reaction

came from Ingrid the saleswoman, Ingrid the connois-
seur or simply from the woman herself.

Equally impossible to judge from his amber eyes was
what Devon was thinking, except she knew that he was
willing her to speak, to show her reaction to this amazing work of art.

'It's... I...' Colleen couldn't find the words and, had
she found them, doubted if she could have spoken them.
Ingrid had no such difficulty.

'Magnificent!' she whispered, making the whisper a
shout. 'Truly it is the finest work you have ever done,
and I must have it for the exhibition. No... I must have
both of them—this and the...fox-woman. They comple-
ment each other...point and counterpoint, darling. Each
can stand alone, of course, but together...truly stagger-
ing! Of course,' she added, 'they will both now overpower everything else in the exhibition, but still...they
must be shown!'

'A bit of an expensive proposition for you if you
can't sell either of them,' he replied, eyes blank now,
revealing nothing of what he really thought of the idea.

Ingrid looked at him, and there was an expression in
her eyes, in her voice, that Colleen couldn't interpret.

'Ah, but will you not sell them, darling?' Ingrid replied, in a tone that seemed strangely prophetic, knowing. 'Are you so sure of that? I think you should not
be. One, at least, you will sell, perhaps both. You must,
I think.'

Colleen heard the message, but it didn't really sink
in. What did, from both remarks, was the drawled, deliberate *darling*, spoken with such casual possessiveness
and confidence...and so obviously accepted by Devon
Burns. The words entered her ears and somehow filtered
down to become lumps of lead in her stomach.

Then Devon was speaking, and his words did little but add to her torment.

'I'd been thinking to keep *Vixen* on display right here in the workshop,' he said, 'just to remind me...'

'To remind you of what? Not to trust? Anyone? Ever? To remain totally a misogynist? Ah, darling, you are not so foolish, I think.'

Ingrid had moved closer to Devon, reaching out to place one perfectly manicured hand on his wrist, forcing him to look at her, to listen. Her tone was firm now, almost callous, but her every gesture cried out her feelings, Colleen thought, her own heart sinking.

'This fox-woman is wonderful work, great work,' said Ingrid. 'But it is history; it is over, finished. And, darling, it is not quite so wonderful as this...' she pointed to the siren '...but this also is finished.'

And then, amazingly, she turned to Colleen, her eyes pleading.

'You must tell him this,' she said. 'He will listen to you.' And Colleen could see how the woman's nails were digging into Devon's arm, how she fairly trembled with emotion.

She, too, was trembling, but only on the inside. The big workshop, which she had found chilly even during the heat of the afternoon, suddenly felt so warm that she thought she might faint. The strong emotions in the room seemed to swarm like clouds of smoke, or bees— dangerous, unpredictable.

Her own feelings were in total confusion; she knew only that Devon Burns *wanted* to retain his ties to the past, to that strange, red-haired woman and her amber-eyed child. And it was equally clear to her that Ingrid's hold on him was just as strong, her need as great as Colleen's own.

Tell him? She could barely think, let alone tell Devon Burns anything, she thought. Not that he would listen anyway; that was a ridiculous assumption. All she really wanted was to escape this place, to flee the tensions and the emotional turmoil, especially her own confused emotions.

Because it was, as Ingrid had said, over, finished. Her part in the work was done and the result was... beautiful? That, certainly, but now she felt only emptiness, a total barrenness of spirit.

'I... I can't tell him anything,' she replied finally, her voice soft, uncertain, almost a whisper, not looking at Devon, not daring to meet his eyes, not really wanting to. 'The pieces are beautiful; they really are. And now it's late and I must go.'

She nearly trampled the dog in her flight, and was outside and reaching to open her car door when Devon caught up with her, his hand like a steel clamp on her arm.

'What's this sudden panic?' he demanded to know. 'Surely you're not *that* upset by the way the siren turned out, are you?'

'No...no, it's absolutely gorgeous, wonderful, perfect,' she replied, waffling, still afraid to meet his eyes. 'I've just...had enough for now, that's all. I've had a really long day and I'm tired and I have a mountain of work waiting for me at home and—'

'And you're being evasive as hell,' he interrupted, pulling her round to face him, using his free hand to lift her chin, to force her to look at him. 'Now, come on, let's have it! What's got you all frothy and defensive and out of sorts?'

'Nothing. As I said, I'm just tired and it's late and I want to go home,' she insisted, trying in vain to free herself and open the door at the same time, succeeding at neither.

'There's more to it than that,' he replied. 'And I'm not letting you go without some sort of sane answer. What is it? Something I've said or done? Or…is it something to do with Ingrid? Honestly, I was as surprised as you when she turned up—although she is prone to that sort of thing, as I guess you must have realised.'

'Oh, yes… I had rather figured *that* out,' Colleen replied, not even bothering to hide the sarcasm in her voice. What did it matter after all? Ingrid had won, assuming that there had even been a contest in the first place. There probably hadn't, she thought; Devon's interest in herself had been restricted to the uses he could find for her, and with the siren finished those were about used up.

This apparently wasn't the 'sort of sane answer' he'd wanted; Devon made no move to release her. Instead he shifted his grip slightly so that she couldn't avoid a closer proximity to him, so that he could not only stare down into her eyes but could also bend close enough for their lips almost to meet, no matter how much Colleen tried to avoid that.

'You're a strange girl,' he murmured, brushing at her lips with his own, their touch almost spark-throwing, alive with his unique brand of magic.

Colleen's insides melted but she struggled against his embrace, struggled even harder against her own desire just to give in to it.

'Perhaps, but one that's going home and doing it now,' she finally managed to gasp when he had finished kissing her. 'You've finished your siren now and you don't need me any more, so I suggest you devote a bit of time to your guest instead of harassing me. I've had about all I'm going to take of your games!'

'Games? You think this is some sort of game?' The look of surprise on his face might have been genuine, but Colleen wasn't about to believe it. After all, she had seen the evidence with her own eyes. She had been made to continue to pose for a sculpture after it had already been finished, she'd been toyed with both physically and emotionally, and now she had just... had...enough!

'Yes,' she said firmly, this time managing to free her arm from his suddenly relaxed grip. 'Yes, I do. Now goodnight!'

This time, perhaps surprisingly, he made no further attempt to stop her from getting into her car. He merely stood there, a look of mild confusion mixed with anger on his handsome face. Then he shrugged, waved one hand in a gesture of defeat—or at least withdrawal.

'Suit yourself,' he said through the open window. 'But you're way off the track, Colleen, if you think I've been playing some complicated bloody game here. Still...'

She didn't hear the rest, didn't want to, couldn't. Even while he was still speaking she yanked the small car into gear and spun away from him, fish-tailing towards the outward driveway and the highway that would lead her home.

It took for ever to get there. The lines on the black bitumen seemed to swim in her tears, and the night highway was alive with possums and wallabies and even an evil-looking Tasmanian devil—all challenging her fickle vision and lack of attention to what she was doing.

She walked into her flat to find the answering machine blinking its imperious command, which she obeyed out of habit. But at the first words in Devon Burns's unmistakable voice she banged the machine off, disconnected it and flung it into the bottom drawer of her desk. Then she turned off the telephone ringer for good measure and swore to herself they would both stay that way until…

'Until for ever!' she cried as she slammed her way to the bedroom, discarding clothing as she went and wishing that she had never met Devon Burns or his damned dog!

The mood persisted into the following morning and grew steadily bleaker through the day. And the next…and the next…and the next… By the following Friday, having forcibly immersed herself in work that seemed fated to go wrong no matter how hard she tried, she was beginning to wonder if turning off the telephone had been such a good idea, but whenever she glanced at its silent, squatting figure Devon Burns's voice echoed in her mind and she restrained herself from turning it back on.

'Not that I'd expect you to phone anyway,' she said to his spectre as it haunted the claustrophobic work room. 'Much less that I'd care; I just don't want to be disturbed, that's all.'

But she had been disturbed—if not by his voice then by visions of him lounging in his hot tub with the lovely blonde Ingrid, touching her…being touched. The worst of such visions had haunted her dreams, where her fickle subconscious had woven reality with threads of total fantasy into painfully erotic nightmares that had brought her bolt upright in bed, yanked from sleep with an abruptness that made any return to it impossible.

One night she'd dreamed that Devon and Ingrid played in the hot tub with floating wooden statues—the werefox, Rooster, her own siren, and others less clear to her dreaming mind's eye—but there had been nothing unclear about the ridicule in their laughter, the cruelty of that ridicule. Colleen had been flung up from sleep to find herself bathed in perspiration, ashamed of her own naïvety, more ashamed of her belief that she ought to have known better right from the start.

In another dream she'd been herself—but trapped in the siren's wooden skin as Burns had pursued her round the workshop with a razor-sharp chisel in his hand while Ingrid had laughed evilly from the steamy safety of the hot tub and Rooster had barked and yodelled his encouragement.

The dreams had been worst in the first few days, but even after that her sleep patterns had tended to be fragmented, as was her appetite. It was too much trouble to cook, not worth the effort to go out and get anything and she was too busy, she told herself, to bother anyway. Coffee followed coffee as she tried to concentrate and failed.

But the coffee wasn't enough to keep her awake indefinitely, although she almost wished that it would, just so that she could be certain not to dream.

She was dozing, head in her arms, at the work table that Friday. Burns's voice began what she thought was just another nightmare—a voice that angrily called out her name between thumping noises that seemed to grow louder and more insistent. There was no Ingrid, no dog, no pictures to heighten the illusion, and Colleen eventually shook herself free, only to realise that it was no illusion at all!

'Damn it, Colleen, answer me; I know you're home and I'm going to talk to you if I have to break this so-

and-so door down,' Burns's voice raged, after yet another thumping session on her front door.

At first bewildered, she stared at the trembling door and then began to tremble herself, looking wildly about for some place to hide from this all too real assault on her warped reality. But to no avail; while her mind was running to hide under the bed her body was moving to obey that gravelly voice.

It wasn't until she actually had her hand on the doorknob that she managed to gather the shards together, to summon an illusion of calm, icy control and pray that she could sustain it long enough to get rid of this man who was the cause of all her torment.

'What do you want?'

Just the right note of reserve, she thought. Distant but not angry, not revealing. Burns looked at her, those damned amber eyes seeing more than she wanted them to see but forestalled by her preparation. He was dressed casually, probably for work, but the plaid shirt was open halfway down his chest and the moleskin trousers might have been painted on him; both revealed poised muscles, tenseness.

'I want to know what the hell's going on,' was the reply in a tone as icy as her own. But his eyes weren't icy; they touched her body like fire everywhere he looked, and they looked *everywhere*, flickering like lightning across her cheeks, her lips, her breasts, down the length of her body and legs.

'Nothing is going on,' she replied, in a voice that sounded mechanical even in her own ears—phoney, faked, but the best she could manage.

'Nothing?' The question was there in the inflection, in the disbelief that almost shouted out with that single, disapproving word.

'No,' she insisted, struggling to follow the conversation, struggling harder to maintain her calmness, her distance. Every time his eyes touched her she felt her mind flinch, but her body responded differently. 'What yare you on about? What are you *doing* here?'

'Are you all right?'

It was as if he hadn't heard her, or didn't intend to pay any attention. Even as he asked the question he was using that muscular body to invade her personal space, to force her backwards through her doorway, following, keeping the distance between them too tight, too intimidating.

'Of course I'm all right. Why shouldn't I be all right? What do you *want*?'

He was inside now, still forcing her backwards, and now his eyes were flickering past her, then back again, revealing everything and yet nothing. She could tell that he was surveying the work room, knew that he was seeing the litter of a week's undisciplined effort—the dirty coffee-cups, the pitifully few unwashed dishes.

'You look like you've been busy.' Not quite a question but it was implied.

'I have been busy,' she replied, calmer now but not really sure why, much less how she was managing it. Burns kept pushing; they were well into the room now, the front door closed, isolating them, trapping…her.

'Is there some law against being busy?' she cried, knowing that her voice was raised, not caring. 'What do you *want*?'

'So busy you don't answer your phone? What's happened to your answering machine?'

'I don't always answer my phone. Especially when I'm working. It doesn't run my life,' she objected. 'And what business is it of yours anyway?'

'You *always* answer your phone when you're working,' he replied. 'And even if you didn't, which I don't believe for a moment, Colleen Ferrar, you'd have the ever ready Bertha, or Freda or whoever, to do it for you. And you haven't! I know because I've been trying to get through to you for a week.'

'My answering machine is bro—' She halted, dumbstruck, as he swerved past her and reached out to snatch up her telephone, eyes travelling unerringly to the ringer switch at 'off'. Then those same eyes turned on her, and they were living question marks. He looked at her, then with frightening accuracy at the bottom drawer of the desk.

'Broken, eh?' he asked in a sarcastic tone, that mobile mouth twisting to emphasise the effect.

'I...it's...it's none of your business,' Colleen stammered as she moved away from him, back towards the doorway. If he dared to open that drawer she didn't know what she would do, and she didn't want to find out.

'It certainly is my business,' he replied, turning to follow her, seeming not to notice her quick breath of relief. 'I told you, Colleen, I've been trying to get you on that telephone for a week! And now I find you've been doing your level best to make sure I was wasting my bloody time. Hell's bells, woman...what am I supposed to think?'

'How about thinking that perhaps I was busy, that I didn't want to be disturbed, that maybe—just maybe—I didn't *want* to talk to you?' Colleen replied, much calmer now that his attention was diverted from the bottom drawer, but still trembling and only able to pray that he wouldn't notice. 'Is that so impossible for you to believe? Or are you convinced that every woman in the world is just waiting with bated breath for your every illustrious word?'

Burns's eyes flashed as if she'd struck him, then as quickly lost their spark, went almost opaque, like sea-worn pieces of broken beer bottle. The effect was startling...and brief. An instant later his mouth quirked in a half-grin and she saw the shadows of amusement dancing behind his eyes.

'I do think you're cranky with me, Colleen,' he said, making no attempt to stem the sarcasm in his voice.

But then he looked round the flat again, and when he looked back at her the sarcasm had gone as quickly as it had come. The expression she could now read was, or could have been if she hadn't known better, concern.

'How long is it since you've eaten?' he asked. 'Properly, I mean—not that sort of goop that bachelor girls throw together when they can't be bothered cooking but don't quite want to starve.'

'So now you're an expert on women's affairs *and* their cooking as well?' she demanded, avoiding his question the only way she could and trying to stifle the surprise it had provoked with its accuracy.

'I'm an expert on all sorts of things,' he replied, and his voice now was strangely quiet, almost frighteningly so. 'Why don't you just answer the question, Colleen?'

'Why should I?'

'Because I asked it. Because it would be polite.'

'You've got your nerve, talking about *polite*. You come pushing your way in here like you own the place, without an invitation, and start giving me the third degree about things that are none of your business, and—'

'Because you haven't had a decent meal for days, I reckon. Probably all hyped up on coffee—and don't deny it; I can see you shaking. You're a mess, woman. Go and sit down while I see what I can do here.'

The words floated over his shoulder as he shifted past her in a movement that would have done a champion footballer proud and stalked into her kitchen, shaking his head at the welter of unwashed dishes, flinging open the refrigerator and shaking his head even harder at the barren interior.

And then—the worst of all! He marched over to peer at the work on her drafting table, flinging papers left and right as he scrutinised them with a disconcerting eye that all too quickly turned upon Colleen herself.

'You're a fool, trying to work like this,' he said. 'No proper food. I'll bet good money you haven't been sleeping right either, and I'm not surprised. How you could ever expect to achieve anything significant going at it this way is a mystery to me…a total mystery. I'd have credited you with more sense than this, Colleen. I'm surprised at you, I really am.'

Colleen didn't know what to say, at first. Her mind was in chaos; about the only certainty she could grasp was that Devon Burns thought that she'd left her phone unanswered and her kitchen a mess because she'd been working too hard. He had no idea about the *real* reasons behind the situation. Now, if she could only keep it that way…

'You're right, of course,' she finally said. 'I… I get carried away like this sometimes and I shouldn't, because, as you know, it doesn't accomplish very much— not really.'

She started edging towards the door. If she could just convince him now, just get him *out* of here…

'I'll stop now, give it a rest—give *me* some rest too,' she said, rambling a bit, willing him to follow. Except that he wasn't moving with her; he was turning away, back into the kitchen.

'Fool,' he was muttering as he once again yanked open the refrigerator, stooping to peer inside and give it a better checking over than the first time.

'What are you doing?' she cried, frustrated now, angry. It had been so close; another moment and he would have been gone, should have been...

'I'm getting ready to fix you some decent tucker—or the best I can manage, anyway,' he replied, haphazardly opening cupboard doors with one hand while he balanced several eggs in the other. 'For a girl with no money problems you do keep a terribly bare larder...you studying to be Old Mother Hubbard or something?'

'But...but I—'

'You've had your chance at it,' he said, with a scowl that changed to half a smile as he plucked a lone tin of mushrooms from the nearly empty pantry. 'Surprised you didn't starve to death on the road to fame and fortune, if this is the way you get things done.'

Colleen was done. She could only watch as he expertly threw together the ingredients for an omelette that eventually arrived in front of her looking so much better than anything she had *ever* cooked—an omelette that made speech impossible because her mouth was watering, her entire being having become fixated upon it.

'You get yourself around that,' he said—almost too late, because Colleen had already succumbed. 'And then it's off to bed with you, because we've got an early start and a very long day ahead tomorrow. You want all the rest you can get.'

'Tomorrow?' She could only mumble the question

around the savoury mouthful of omelette, but the panic in her mind obviously didn't get to her voice.

'Your memory playing up too?' he asked, Smiling, too calm, too sure of himself. 'You *have* been working too hard, Colleen. The change'll be good for you.'

He paused, but she was still chewing frantically when he continued without giving her a chance to interrupt.

'Tomorrow's Rooster's big day...remember? His first all-age competition—the one we've been training for, with your help on occasion. Surely you wouldn't miss that?'

'I thought you didn't want me there,' she finally managed to say, still struggling with the immense feeling of relief that he didn't realise the effect he was having on her. He must *not* realise it—and would not if she could have her way. If she could only convince him just to go away and leave her alone; she was too tired, too stressed out, too vulnerable.

'I remember saying I hoped he wouldn't play up because of you being there,' Burns admitted, only to add, 'But I also remember—specifically—inviting you to come along this weekend.'

'But why?'

'Because I thought you'd be interested, of course. And if you aren't—you should be! It doesn't matter now; you're coming anyway, just for *my* peace of mind. I want to be able to concentrate on Rooster. I'll have to. And I wouldn't be able to concentrate on him and worry about you at the same time.'

'You don't have to worry about me,' Colleen retorted around another mouthful of omelette. 'Why should you have to?'

Burns scowled, then turned the scowl into a broad look of disdain as he swept it round the flat, his amber eyes touching almost fastidiously on the dirty dishes, the scattered working papers, the general mess of the place. Then he turned the scowl upon *her* with much the same attitude.

'Look at yourself—you look like death warmed up,' he said, without so much as a smile to lighten the criticism. 'You've obviously been working too hard, haven't been taking proper care of yourself, and if left to your own devices you'd keep right on doing it until you dropped from sheer exhaustion. And don't bother to argue, Colleen Ferrar; I know you too well for that to work.

'No, you're going to bed in a few minutes, and first thing tomorrow you're coming with me and you're going to *stay* with me for the rest of the weekend. *No work*! If you get too bored, you can find a tree somewhere to sleep under; at least I'll know you're getting some rest.'

Colleen couldn't argue. The words weren't there because she hadn't had any opportunity to prepare an argument. She'd forgotten his invitation, or ignored it in the heat of her annihilation by Ingrid, and now she could only sit there with her mouth full and stare blankly at him, half of her wanting to scream at him to get out of her life and stop tormenting her, the other half wanting just to sit and cry.

She could only continue eating the omelette, wondering how something that had tasted so wonderful to begin with was now beginning to taste horribly like ashes. But she didn't dare stop, because Devon Burns was watching, willing her to eat every last bite or suffer the consequences. She hadn't the slightest doubt that he'd force her to eat if the notion crossed his mind.

Her suspicions grew even larger, however, when she

finally did finish the omelette. Burns reached across the table and picked up her plate, waving with his other hand towards the bedroom.

'Right. Off to bed with you, my lady. I'll just give this place a quick cleanup and then come and tuck you in if you're awake enough to need it, which I doubt.'

'I...but...I...' She tried desperately but somehow couldn't quite find the right words to tell him that she could put herself to bed without his help, and that what she really wanted him to do was just go...get out.

'Oh, all right. I'll even kiss you goodnight if it'll make you happy,' he said, deliberately misinterpreting her confusion and grinning mischievously as he did so. 'But nothing more—unless you're prepared to beg and plead a little.'

Then he laughed wickedly at her expression of distaste, and stayed watching as she self-consciously moved towards her bedroom, unable to keep from looking back at him with what Colleen knew had to be an expression of caution.

'Don't forget to brush your teeth,' was his final word as she closed the door behind her and stood there, knees trembling, almost sick with the certainty that however she ought to have handled this situation she'd done it wrong!

The feeling intensified when she found the courage to look at herself in the bathroom mirror—hair a ratty mess, eyes puffy and red with deep dark circles under them.

'You look worse than death warmed over, my girl,' she muttered, and immediately squared her shoulders and decided—not before time, with hindsight—that enough was enough. 'Brushing teeth can wait until after a shower,' she told the haggard image, not bothering to ponder whether the goodnight kiss threat had sponsored the change in attitude.

Burns hardly looked round when she peered through the door and advised him of the decision. He had already run the washing-up water and was elbow-deep in the sink with every dirty dish in the place stacked up beside him. He didn't even bother to reply, merely nodded his acceptance of the announcement and returned to his domestic chores, whistling dismally and off-key as he did so.

Colleen retreated to the steamy warmth of the shower and the sweet scents of soap and shampoo. She stayed in longer than she had intended—stayed until she was half-asleep there on her feet. Then she wrapped her hair in a towel turban and her body in the most decorous nightgown she owned, and tucked herself deep into the bed with the covers pulled close up beneath her chin.

And tried to stay awake long enough for the arrival of the promised goodnight kiss, unable to keep from wondering if Burns would leave it at that. He'd given her no time but 'early' for their morning departure and was more than capable, she knew only too well, of deciding to spend the night himself on her lounge sofa or even, should the fancy strike him, in bed with her.

Colleen shivered deliciously at the thought, but the shiver quickly transformed itself to a yawn and the thought drifted into a vacuum that she snuggled into gratefully. Whatever Devon's plan, she wasn't going to be awake for it.

That thought took her into a dreamless sleep; what brought her out of it to face the cold light of dawn was something quite different altogether.

CHAPTER NINE

His breath was warm against her cheek, and Colleen, less than half-awake, was content just to lie there, letting her imagination float on that softness, the warmth of it, the gentleness.

He had promised a tucking-in, half threatened a goodnight kiss to go with it. Ridiculous, of course. He didn't really care for her, certainly didn't love her as she now realised she loved him. But did that matter...just for now...?

His warm breath paused, then resumed. Colleen snuggled closer into the covers, surreptitiously exposing more of her neck, already fancying that she could feel the first cool touch of his lips, her body warm, cosy, relaxed...receptive.

Her last waking thought had involved a sort of blind acceptance, a sureness that if this opportunity came she would just go with it, just take whatever she could of him for as long as she could—not much better than the nothing she'd come home with a week earlier, but better, a little bit better. And if that was all there was, all there could be...

She had a moment's hesitation then, wishing that she had put on her most seductive nightgown rather than the most sedate, and reached one hand up to the high neckline in a reflexive gesture.

Burns's hot breath was like a summer wind now, moving along her neck, laying a track for his lips to follow. Colleen sighed heavily, soulfully, as she felt that wind along her forearm, felt his moist tongue licking at her fingers.

She reached out to touch him, to run her fingers along the strong lines of his jaw, his cheek, heard his low growl of pleasure as her fingers felt—

Fur! Her eyes opened, still half expecting to find Burns's amber eyes only inches from her own. They were eyes, and they were amber—but they weren't the eyes of a lover!

Colleen's shriek was half terror, half indignant outrage. Rooster flung himself away from her, his flailing tail knocking over the bedside clock-radio, his scrambling claws churning the bedside rug into a heap that tripped her as she leapt out of bed in pursuit. Somewhere in the kitchen she heard a pan drop with a metallic clatter, then Burns's voice as he yelled at the astonished dog.

'Rooster! You fool of a hound; get out of that!'

Colleen had her hand on the doorknob when it was suddenly flung against her and she found herself—now!—meeting Devon Burns's amber eyes—eyes alive with concern, surprise and just enough amusement that she couldn't help but notice.

'Are you all right?'

Strong hands reached out to catch her by the shoulders, steadying her and yet somehow managing to caress her at the same time.

'All right?' she cried. 'What do *you* think? What is that dog doing in my bedroom? What are *you* doing?'

'I *was* cooking breakfast,' he replied, relaxing his fingers, allowing her to writhe free of his supporting grip.

Colleen stumbled yet again on the crumpled rug, caught herself, flung out an arm against his reach to steady her yet again. She glared up at him, her fury enhanced by the stolid calm he projected.

'Breakfast?' She was shrieking; her voice echoed through the sudden closeness of the room, but she didn't care, hardly even noticed.

Burns shrugged. 'It seemed like a good idea at the time,' he said. 'But my timing's to hell; you'll have to wait now while I have another go at the eggs—the ones I dropped when you screamed won't be much chop now. Rooster'll like them th—'

'I'll kill him! What is that dog *doing* in here? What are *you* doing in here?'

'Making breakfast, like I said,' he replied, eyes truly laughing now, although his voice was unreasonably calm. 'As for him—well, I guess it's my fault. I looked in on you a few minutes ago and I guess I didn't shut the door properly.'

Colleen shook her head, totally confused, yet suddenly conscious of how she must look—hair a mess, no make-up, her eyes puffy from sleep. She looked down at her nightgown and *now* was glad of her choice; at least she was covered!

'I...you...' She floundered, stammered, stopped. Burns's mobile lips were forming into a subtle grin, his eyes shining as he looked at her, shaking his head.

'You want to go and get dressed or something,' he said gently. 'I'll just clean up my mess and get some more eggs going and we'll eat. You'll feel better then.'

Already he was turning away, then, as suddenly, turned back to drop a totally unexpected kiss on her cheek before she could stop him, before she even knew what was happening.

'Five minutes. OK?'

Colleen was left standing there, trembling in her emotional confusion but able only to stare at the door he'd closed—firmly this time—behind him.

She heard his voice faintly as he said, 'You can help me clean up, you fool of a dog, and then it's outside with you. I don't think either of us is very popular, but you, my lad, had best be outside and safe in the truck before she comes out, or it'll be roast Rooster for brekkie and no mistake.'

The soft whuffle of reply was only just audible, but it was enough!

'Get that animal out of here!' she screamed as she turned and fled to the bathroom, wishing that she hadn't been able to hear Burns's chuckle of amusement at the outburst.

The dog was gone when she finally emerged into the living area of the flat, more flustered now than actually angry, but determined that she had endured quite enough of Devon Burns and his damned dog. The dog was gone, but the master remained. And the air was redolent with the scent of freshly perked coffee and breakfast cooking.

At the very least she was halfway presentable now. She had put on a fleecy sweatshirt and tracksuit pants and taken some effort to tame her rowdy hair. Burns wore what he'd had on the night before, and if he'd slept in those clothes he must have done so very carefully, because he looked extremely fresh and tidy for this ludicrous hour of the morning.

'Steak and eggs OK?' Burns asked, turning from his post at the stove to greet her with a smile, with laughing amber eyes that swiftly roved over the landscape of her body from tousled hair to slippered toes. 'I did just a bit of bacon too, if you fancy it, and there's some not bad croissants.'

Colleen could only stare at the sparkling kitchen, the table laid out for their breakfast even to the inclusion of a sprig of flowers in a jamjar vase. She didn't know what to say, didn't honestly know if she wanted to say anything at all. The place looked as if he'd spent the entire night house-cleaning, but...

'I made a midnight run for tucker,' he said with a shrug. 'Can't go dog-trialing on an empty stomach, and you don't exactly keep what anybody'd call a well-stocked larder, you know.'

She numbly followed his gesture, allowed herself to be seated at the table, sat in silence as he quickly and competently forked steak, eggs, bacon and tomato onto a plate and set it before her, then poured coffee into the cup at her place.

'Get going on that,' he said. 'I won't be a minute.' And he was turning away to begin filling a plate for himself, having poured his own coffee after that. Colleen looked at Burns, then at her plate, then gave in to the rumblings of her tummy and the delectable odours emanating from the food.

Across from her Burns also ate in silence, though his eyes strayed across the table to rest upon her, and she fancied that he was hiding a niggling smile behind those eyes.

It wasn't until they'd finished eating and he'd poured them a second coffee that either of them spoke, and it was he who began, with a totally unexpected, hardly believable comment.

'Of course, you realise you can't expect this kind of service every day of the week.'

It made no sense, but the gentle seriousness of the comment gave Colleen pause; she found herself poised with her coffee-cup in her hand halfway to her mouth, eyes locked with his and a feeling of illogical apprehension sitting on top of the food inside her.

'I can't imagine why I would,' she finally managed to say. 'But isn't that sort of a…profound statement for this insane hour of the morning?'

'Only five-thirty,' he responded, but something had changed behind those amber eyes. She could feel rather than actually see that he was thinking, and thinking rather hard.

The silence resumed, but now it was accompanied by an atmosphere of what could only be described as mutual suspicion, caution, as each of them sipped at their coffee and stared at each other.

And again it was Burns who broke the silence, this time in a voice tinged with caution, a voice so soft as to be hardly audible, yet so vibrant, so alive that it reflected the inner tension she could see in his every gesture, every word.

'Just as a matter of interest, Colleen, how long has your answering machine been broken?' he asked.

She paused before replying. To lie or just to…bend the truth a little bit: that was the question now—and she didn't much like either option. Something told her that this was no time to play games, and yet she was equally certain that that was exactly what Devon Burns was doing.

'It…isn't actually broken,' she finally replied. 'I just…well…haven't been using it—that's all.'

'Yes, I know that,' he replied enigmatically. 'But…' he looked significantly towards the telephone '…then where is it?'

'I put it away.'

'You put it away.' Not a question, not an answer. Just a comment, accompanied by a not so subtle raising of one dark eyebrow as he looked again to where the machine should have been sitting beside the phone.

'Is there some law against that?'

Colleen was being defensive and she knew it, but she was damned if she was going to let him totally dominate her.

'Of course not,' he said. 'Except that...well...can I ask *when* you put it away? Or, more correctly, *when* did you use it last?'

'Does it matter?'

'I wouldn't be asking if I didn't think so.' And now his eyes were dark amber pools that seemed to be drawing her closer, mesmerising her.

'Since I started on this latest project,' Colleen replied evasively, hoping that she didn't sound evasive but certain she did.

Burns said nothing, just sat there with his eyes fixed on her and his expressive hands folded across his chest. The look he gave her was speculative but not easy to interpret—deliberately so, Colleen suspected.

Finally he growled deep in his throat and then said, 'OK, let's do it your way, an inch at a time. Dear Ms Ferrar—was your answering machine working/in use/operative/in service the evening you returned from your last modelling session with me? How's that for specific?'

'I haven't used it since then.'

'Which does *not* answer my question.'

'Don't shout at me,' she snapped, in a vain attempt to disguise her guilt. 'This is *my* house, I'll remind you.'

'Why, so it is.' His voice was like silk, but the devils behind his eyes pranced and danced gleefully. Colleen couldn't help feeling that his trap was silken too, like that of some great spider. She couldn't keep meeting those interrogating eyes; they saw too much, *knew* too much. And yet…she was damned if she was going to make this easy for him.

'Let's try this another way,' he was saying, and she was all too aware of his movements as he rose to pour them fresh coffee while he spoke, drawing out the words to fit his graceful movements. 'Now listen carefully, because I don't want you to fudge this one. On the evening you last modelled for me, on your return home, here, did you or did you not find a message waiting for you upon said answering machine? And did you or did you not listen to that message before said answering machine ceased to work or was brutally slain or fell or was pushed or whatever the hell happened to the damn thing?'

The last few words emerged with machine-gun precision as he slammed his muscular body down into his chair and leaned on the table in front of him, demanding a reply, insisting even.

Colleen had never seen such rigidly controlled temper. Burns looked as if the wrong word would set him off in a fury. And she had no real choice of words.

'Not.' She got the word out, but only just, and when it did emerge it was in the barest of whispers.

'Ah.' His reply was in an even softer whisper; the mighty breath that swelled his chest was probably louder. So was the grinding of his teeth, the drumming of strong fingers on the table beside his coffee-cup.

The drumming was a thunder in the silence between them; the look in his eyes was a thunder of a different sort, as was the sound of Colleen's own heart thudding in her ears. And they all went on…and on…and on… Until he said again, 'Ah,' and looked down at his hands, then back at her, down at his fingers again, then around the room in a vague yet also specific way.

Colleen didn't dare move. Her mouth was too dry to speak, her fingers too unsteady in her lap for her to even *think* of trying to pick up her cooling coffee. She tried to follow his glances but couldn't quite manage it.

'You were…a bit surprised, then,' he finally said, 'when I showed up last night. Yes, I suppose you were.' That comment was as vague as his appraisal of the room, but what followed was anything but!

'Colleen—*where* is your answering machine?'

'I told you, I put it away.'

'Where?'

'Does it matter?'

'*Where?*' His voice said that it did indeed matter.

'In…in a drawer.' She was almost afraid to answer. Devon's jaw was clenched; his rangy, muscular body was so tense that she thought he was going to explode. The atmosphere in the room was no less tense; she could almost *see* the sparks in the glare that those amber eyes were shooting at her.

Then, quicksilver swift, his attitude changed. He took one huge breath and relaxed, deflating—no, not deflating, just easing into the sort of calm-before-the-storm posture of some great hunting cat. Even his voice had a sort of purr when he finally spoke.

'You didn't listen to any messages when you got back that night,' he mused, 'and you haven't used the machine since. So the tape's still in it, along with whatever messages might be on it. Is that a fair assumption?'

Colleen didn't answer, couldn't. She just sat there and stared back at him, knowing that she was perched on the edge of his trap now, and also certain that no matter what she said, what she did, it was going to be wrong—for her!

'Well?'

Colleen sat. Burns sat. Her body was tense with suspicion and apprehension. His was even more so, but his tension was that of a predatory animal at the end of the stalk.

'What time does this dog trial start?' It was a frail attempt and she knew it, but she also knew enough about gundog trials to *hope* that she might divert his attention. Check-ins were rigidly controlled; one was on time or out of the competition.

Burns said nothing, merely shook his head. Almost sadly, she thought, but not as sadly as she was beginning to feel. Colleen started up out of her chair, picking up the dirty dishes as she did so. Burns, to her astonishment, did likewise; they arrived at the sink side by side.

'You want to wash or dry?' he said, not even bothering to hide the chuckle in his voice, that infuriating cocksure attitude he handled so well.

'I would have thought we could just leave them,' Colleen said, frantic now for any ruse that might work. 'After all, we can't afford to be late and it's getting—'

'Getting awful close to crunch time, eh, Ms Ferrar?' His voice was silky soft; the lean, hard body so close to her own was anything but.

'How about we just do these dishes *now*?' he asked, in a whisper that was almost ghastly in its softness. 'You wash—I'll put things away. I know where everything goes now.'

Colleen couldn't help it. She turned to glare furiously into eyes that returned her glare with mocking highlights of laughter, her gasp of fury blunted by a voice that growled and caressed in the same words.

'You're *so* beautiful.''

But before the words had actually registered he was turning away to stack the dishes in the sink and turn on the water, one hand flicking the mixer tap as the other generously squeezed out detergent into the streaming water.

Colleen stood there, bedazzled by the sheer insanity of it all, until Burns finished running the water and turned to take her forearms in his strong fingers, gently but irresistibly shifting her towards the sudsy sink. Only when she shrugged him away and plunged her hands into the water of her own volition did he release her, and his grin was a model of self-satisfaction before he plucked up the teatowel and turned away.

'You do a good job now,' he muttered, but didn't stop to watch. Colleen could only stand there, up to her elbows in suds, as he strode quickly across to the phone stand and with uncanny but not unexpected accuracy yanked open the bottom drawer and lifted out the answering machine.

'Poor Freda,' he crooned, lifting the machine like some grisly trophy. 'What a thing to do to you—locked up there in the dark like a criminal…she ought to be ashamed of herself.'

And the triumphant, gleeful look he shot at Colleen was evidence that he would make very, very sure that she would be!

'To think that you once dared to chastise me for the way I talked about poor old Ignatius,' he said to Colleen, shaking his head in mock dismay as those long, slender fingers flew through the intricacies of plugging the machine in, attaching the various connections. Colleen heard the hiss-click of the machine spinning into readiness, saw the single red eye, as accusing as the two amber ones he turned on her.

Then he was back beside her, moving so swiftly that she saw only a blur of movement through the mist of tears she couldn't quite control.

'Right, love, let's get on with the washing-up,' he growled. 'We'll clear up the dishes, and then we'll clear up one or two or three other little things, and then...'

The rest was left unsaid, the threat simply but effectively implied. Colleen couldn't handle the expression in those eyes; she stared down into the suds and began doing as she was told, her fingers moving sluggishly, her mind racing a million miles an hour in a million different directions.

Beside her, Burns was a silent, omnipresent body, his muscular thigh occasionally touching her hip, his elbow occasionally brushing her own, and his damnably agile fingers so quick to catch utensils that she was about to drop—the cup she fumbled, the plate that slipped from her fingers.

All in silence—a silence that grew and was magnified until it roared like the futile, silent scream inside her as he imposed his will upon her, using these casual touches to reinforce the imprinting of past lovemaking, past intimacies.

Colleen didn't look at him, could hardly even focus on what she was doing. She merely manoeuvred her hands through the task he'd set her, enduring, trying to drum up whatever reserves of strength she might still have.

'All done?'

She nodded blankly, then obeyed his instruction to pull the plug, stood there silently as the water and suds swished themselves away and half wished that she could do likewise, especially when he turned her gently round and began to dry off her hands, making the drying of each finger a singular, separate event.

'Now come and we'll sit down somewhere comfortable,' he said, and his voice was seductively hypnotic, like his touch. Colleen felt his hands at her waist as he guided her to the sofa, allowed herself to be manipulated, to be placed just *so*, felt him sit down beside her but didn't dare now to meet his eyes, just…couldn't.

Her eyes closed. She felt a finger beneath her chin, lifted her head obediently but couldn't open her eyes, didn't want to. Heard his voice whisper-soft.

'Relax, love. Just relax and I'll tell you a story or two. All you have to do is listen, and when I'm done we'll *both* listen to what Freda has to tell us. It's been long enough; I'm rather curious myself, to tell you the truth.'

Colleen started to reply, but his lips were there to halt her, there to touch lightly on her own, perfectly matched to mould her lips, to hold her mouth in enforced silence.

'Not now,' he whispered through the kiss. Then he added, 'Later. Plenty of time for questions later.'

All the time in the world, she realised. His very next words assured her of that—words he would repeat often, use to punctuate the other things he had to tell her—things that weren't important any longer but things he wanted to tell her, so she listened.

But the important words were the first ones, three of them.

'I love you,' he said. 'Believe that first.'

Colleen held on to those words as if they were a prayer, almost needed to. Everything Devon Burns had to say was so incredible, some of it so totally unexpected, that she had trouble believing that she was really awake, really hearing his words, feeling the touch of his delicate fingers at her cheek, on her throat, her wrist.

He loved *her*. Not Ingrid, not the striking redhead with the child who as startlingly resembled Burns himself, but *her*!

And he'd told her earlier too. Except that she hadn't listened to that final message on her answering machine, and had spent more than a week in a bleak despair that had been totally, astonishingly unnecessary.

But now he was telling her again. And would keep on telling her, he said, until she finally got it through her head, until she stopped fighting him, stopped finding excuses to deny it—had she ever done that? she wondered—until she admitted that this was what she wanted, what they both wanted.

'You've been driving me crazy all week,' he said. 'At first I thought I was wrong, that you didn't share my feelings after all. Then I thought, OK, I'd have to accept that. But I couldn't, Colleen, not without hearing you say it, *seeing* you say it. And every day I'd phone, and phone, and then I began to wonder if you'd packed up and left the country, or if you were sick, or… Well, hell…I thought all sorts of weird and wonderful things.

'Until finally I couldn't take any more of it. I *had* to know, one way or the other. And then when I got here and it looked like you'd just got super-involved in some work project I could have broken your lovely neck.'

Burns sighed, reaching up with fingers like spun silk to touch at her neck, to stroke rainbows along her throat and down into the hollows of her collarbone.

'But I couldn't. You looked so worn out and frazzled that all I wanted to do was take care of you.' Then his mouth nuzzled into her throat and he growled through his kisses, 'Until I realised this morning that you hadn't even *listened* to the message I left—then I wanted to break your neck again. But now I've got a better punishment in mind—an appropriate one even.'

He shifted so as to be able to look her squarely in the eye, and laughed.

'I am going to take you into your little trundle-bed, Colleen, and make love to you as it has never, ever been done before. I am going to kiss you and touch you and *show* you exactly how I feel about you, and I'm not going to stop until you absolutely beg for mercy. And until you can admit to both of us how you feel about me too.' And he laughed again, wickedly, wonderfully. 'But not until *after* the dog trial's over today.

'Problem is—I expect *I'll* suffer more from waiting than you will.' And he grinned. 'I usually suffer anyway with that damned dog. This might just be a pleasant change.'

CHAPTER TEN

COLLEEN shivered with delicious anticipation as Burns's lean, strong fingers stroked her arch, not only tickling her foot but sending tendrils of ecstasy the length of her leg. And beyond. She shivered again as his lips touched at her ankle-bone, his teeth nicking gently at the sensitive skin below it.

'You taste delicious,' he said. 'All soapy and steamy.'

'And I still think you had this planned from the start,' she replied, not opening her eyes, merely drinking in the sensation that his other hand created as it glided higher along the inside of her thigh.

'Hoped, not planned.' Then he chuckled, his lips giving the most astonishing effect against her water-softened skin. 'Well...maybe just a bit of planning.'

'I'm pleased to see you admit it,' Colleen retorted, 'considering I have it all on tape as evidence.'

'Which I suppose you'll hold against me in the long run,' he replied, lips now moving further up the leg which he'd lifted from the steaming waters of the hot tub. 'Do you think that's fair? After all, you didn't even bother to listen to your answering machine—for a week, I might remind you!—until I insisted on it. If I hadn't insisted, you still wouldn't know how I feel about you—or at least you mightn't believe it, which is the same thing.'

Nor would she have. Even having been told, even having been shown in a thousand and one delightful ways, she still felt as if it was all a dream, a unique fantasy in which all her senses had been heightened to overload and beyond.

'Oh, I'm sure you'd have found some way to get your message across,' she replied, unwilling even now to admit how difficult she found it to believe that it was really happening. Then she sighed at the wonder of his manipulating fingers on a body she would have thought already sated with his lovemaking. But he knew better, and continued to prove it.

'Besides, I thought you were busy with Ingrid. You never gave me any reason to believe—'

'You're blind, that's all. I did everything but shout it from the roof-tops, and very nearly did that too,' he growled. 'And let's drop this rubbish about Ingrid, all right? Give me credit for some sense, at least. You should like Ingrid, actually. *She* didn't have trouble sorting out how I felt about you—she spent the rest of her visit rousting on me to rush into Launceston and get *us* sorted out.' Whereupon he chuckled. 'All in the name of my art, of course; Ingrid always did have rather specific priorities.'

'Of which you were very, very high on the list,' Colleen replied. 'And not entirely because of your art. You must be blind if you haven't realised by now she fancies you like crazy.'

'I've already got a mother,' was the reply, slightly muffled by the fact that his lips were busy exploring her knee while his hands did even more interesting things keeping it in place for just that purpose. 'That woman would have an artist chained to his work for eternity; she has the soul of a slave-driver.'

'More likely chained to the...well...never mind,' Colleen said, now quite happy to drop the subject. She personally would always be convinced of Ingrid's *real* hopes for Devon Burns, but if he chose not to see them she wasn't fool enough to keep insisting. Instead she changed the subject entirely.

'Didn't Rooster do wonderfully today? I thought he was a real champion.'

'Half a champion,' Burns muttered distractedly. 'He'll need another big win to get his championship.' The words were slightly indistinct because he was kissing her all along the length of her leg as he spoke.

'Well, at least you can't accuse me of distracting him,' Colleen insisted, writhing in the warm water, herself almost driven to distraction by what he was doing.

'Not of distracting him, but you sure as blazes distracted me,' was the muffled reply. 'I'm convinced now that I was the *only* one to suffer that punishment I promised you. Stupid idea, putting this off while we went to that damned dog trial.'

'It was your idea after all,' she sighed, not quite willing to admit that she had been *at least* as punished by the self-enforced delay as he had been. 'I had thought the whole business of the trial was just an excuse for you to come and harass me for not answering your message.' She could say that—now.

'I didn't *need* an excuse; I came to find out how it was I could leave you such a splendid, loving answering-machine message and be totally ignored! You came very close to doing serious injury to my fragile ego,' Burns muttered, without any slowing of his caresses.

Colleen was surprised that he'd bothered to come after a week with no response. It must have taken a great deal of courage, she thought.

The message on the answering machine had contained none of his earlier humorous banter, no Ignatius and Freda exchanging innuendo. It had been a blatantly frank admission of love, of caring, of needing, ending with the message that he had several things to tidy up businesswise and would be arriving that weekend to take her to the dog trial.

Had she bothered to listen—and she now found it difficult to imagine being so stubborn, so totally unsure of her own feelings that she hadn't!—she would have turned around and driven back to him as fast as her car could have made the journey.

'And as for that damned dog he's already won the highest prize he'll ever get for retrieving; he brought me *you*. Nothing he could do now would ever manage to top that.'

'He should be lying by the fire with a champion bone,' Colleen said. 'It isn't fair really. He won the trial for you and now he's out there in a cold, lonely kennel, and we're—'

'And we're where I've wanted us to be for longer than I like to admit,' he replied, after he'd used his mobile mouth to interrupt and stop her talking. 'Now stop rabbiting on about Rooster. I know he's wonderful and all that, but he's not a person—even though he sometimes thinks he is. He's a dog and he's happy being a dog…and *this*…is no place…for a dog.'

The words were interspersed with kisses that touched like small flames along the length of her leg. 'And *I*, in case you haven't noticed, am a man. A man with very specific needs just at this moment.'

'You can't want *more*, surely?' she teased, only to have him growl against her skin. 'Is this more of your punishment?'

'Call it that if you like. There's all sorts of punishments, my love. Like this. And this again…and again and again.'

And she shivered as his fingers traced patterns in the soapsuds along her leg, leaving a trail for his lips to follow. Colleen writhed with delight, threatening to make the steaming hot tub overflow.

Devon was immersed to the point where even his strong, muscular shoulders were covered, but those incredible amber eyes laughed at her. No, she decided, not *at* her, but *with* her.

'You wait until tomorrow, when you're standing around in the cold grey light of dawn, with the wind blowing like it did today—like it always does at that trial site,' he said. 'You'll be thinking this was heaven then.'

'I think it's heaven now,' Colleen sighed, then gasped as he tugged her closer against him, lifting her so that his lips could capture a nipple, so that his tongue could tease it into a fragile peak of sensitivity.

His hand moved too, further up the inside of her thigh, fingers delicately fluttering against her skin, increasing her readiness as they neared their goal. The sensation was exquisite, tantalising, the sweetest of tortures. Again Colleen gasped.

'Are you really going to let Ingrid take both those pieces to Europe—for sale?' she asked some time later as she lay in his arms, her entire body tingling in the aftermath of their lovemaking.

'She'll be getting *Vixen* for sure,' he said, mouth close to her ear, making even this almost irrelevant discussion an act of love. 'I was going to keep it just to remind me how damned fickle and illogical women can be, but now that I've got you—'

The splash of water against his face stopped him only briefly, but the gesture earned her a kiss before he continued.

'Be serious for a minute, because that bit of work had a lot to do with shaping my attitudes—especially towards this business of working on commissions,' he said. 'As I guess I told you earlier, it was the first *real* commission I ever undertook—and the last as well. I always had a *feeling* that it wasn't the way I ought to work, but when my cousin Dave asked I needed the money. I let myself down by going against my own better judgement...and I ended up paying the price.'

'Your *cousin*? You never told me that.'

'Oh, not really a cousin. A sort of fourth cousin thrice removed. Let's just say a distant relative. He's got more money than brains and more brains than taste, especially in women, but he wanted me to do a statue of his *darling* wife, and *Vixen* was the result.'

'And she didn't like it—so much so that she's hated you ever since?'

'What she mostly didn't like was the fact that all I wanted to do was carve and she had...other ideas,' he replied quietly. 'And, of course, she's as mad as a meat-axe—which *nobody* knew at the time. But yes, I suppose she also didn't like the end result either. I didn't really see, at first, just how much of her true nature was revealed: the feral quality of the woman...and the madness! Sometimes my hands work better than my eyes. But I guess *she* did, and then she told Dave a pack of bull-dust that had him fairly frothing for a while.

'In the end she got her revenge, which was to ensure the work wouldn't be exhibited, but she still hates me.

Not that I care all that much, but it certainly did a lot to make me gun-shy about commissions.'

He paused, but only for a moment. 'And it also, with the benefit of hindsight, explains why I was so dead-set on you not seeing *Siren* before it was done—and why I was so worried about your reaction to it. I don't know what I'd have done if you'd gone all strange and decided you didn't like it, or...well...whatever.'

'Your cousin—which explains why the little boy looks so much like...' Colleen was musing without really being aware of it.

'There's not much danger of him getting lost in this end of the state,' Burns said. 'The family resemblance is so strong that I wonder—now that I've seen him—what Lucinda contributed at all. I just hope it wasn't her temperament, or her madness! From all I hear through the family grapevine, it seems that he's a quite decent kid and she treats him OK too, especially now she's under treatment.'

'I... I sort of wondered, that night in the ice-cream parlour, if maybe he wasn't...'

'Mine?' He chuckled, then leaned down to kiss her. 'I had a feeling you were thinking that, but it didn't seem like the time to go into it. It was a fair enough assumption, after all; I've got a picture of me at that age around somewhere and I could be his twin.'

'You knew! And you deliberately let me go on thinking that?'

'What was I supposed to do—deny it when you hadn't even asked? You wouldn't have believed me anyway...not then. We hardly even knew each other, my love.'

'I'm not sure I ought to even now,' she said, not really meaning it but unable to resist the chance to stir him. 'You're an extremely deceitful person—look at the way you had me continue to pose for a sculpture that you had finished earlier. I really think,' she said, wriggling closer into his arms to show that she wasn't *that* serious, 'that I probably ought to be quite insulted...being asked to pose, at least towards the end, for the sculpture of a *dog*!'

'At least it was a male dog; you'd really have grounds for complaint if I'd been using you as the model for a bitch,' he growled in her ear, and laughed when she attempted to dunk him.

'And while we're on the subject of *deceitful*,' he said, after using his longer reach and greater strength to gather Colleen against him where she couldn't retaliate, 'I demand an apology this very instant. It's a blatant case of the pot calling the kettle black—and you can't do anything but admit it, my love, because you've been convicted out of your own very pretty mouth.'

'Convicted of what? You *are* deceitful.'

'Says she who promised never to snoop and finally succumbed to her own feminine curiosity. You did, Colleen, and that doesn't surprise me as much as hearing you admit it.'

'I admit nothing,' she retorted, wriggling in his grasp to no real effect. 'I don't even know what you're talking about.'

She was turned around now, so that avoiding those amber eyes was impossible, not that she wanted to— until he explained. Then she wanted to dunk herself, perhaps permanently.

'I'm talking about what you've already admitted,' he said with a smug grin. 'That you're a snoop, Colleen Ferrar-soon-to-be-Burns.' And he proceeded to tickle her—to great effect—in a place where she was definitely not used to being tickled.

'You might as well admit it; we can't start our married life with something like that hanging over your head,' he said, laughing at her discomfort. 'If you *didn't* snoop how could you have known I was working on the Rooster piece while you were posing?'

'Because I snooped, of course, which I suspect is exactly what I was intended to do,' she said then. 'In fact, I *know* that's what I was intended to do; you set me up!'

Burns merely laughed. 'No, my love, I didn't,' he said. 'I only had that piece there because I had to have something to do with my hands while you were posing, or there'd have been all sorts of problems. In fact I didn't remember which piece was where until almost the last minute, and you'd laugh yourself if you'd seen the scurrying around I had to do, getting things swapped round while I was bringing in Ingrid's bags.'

His grin then was pure boyish mischief.

'But it was worth it to see the look on your face when it came time to unveil *Siren*; you were just *so* certain of what you were going to see...'

'It's not funny.' Colleen finally was able to reply. 'You, the great professional, taking advantage like that.'

'It was just that I didn't know any better way to keep you where I could keep an eye on you.' His fingers, meanwhile, kept tracing intricate patterns along her flank. 'I don't suppose it's any consolation to know I had the devil's own time trying to keep it *just* to looking and not…this…'

His mouth descended to halt any protest, any attempt to argue further. His kiss was gentle, his lips perfectly shaped to take in the contours of her mouth, practised now in melding their individual ardour into a single, elemental passion.

'None at all,' she managed to whisper after an interval that seemed an eternity, but which they both knew was only the beginning.

HARLEQUIN PRESENTS

HARLEQUIN PRESENTS
men you won't be able to resist
falling in love with...

HARLEQUIN PRESENTS
women who have feelings
just like your own...

HARLEQUIN PRESENTS
powerful passion in
exotic international settings...

HARLEQUIN PRESENTS
intense, dramatic stories that will keep you
turning to the very last page...

HARLEQUIN PRESENTS
The world's bestselling romance series!

Harlequin® Historical

From rugged lawmen and
valiant knights to defiant heiresses
and spirited frontierswomen,
Harlequin Historicals will
capture your imagination with
their dramatic scope, passion
and adventure.

Harlequin Historicals...
they're too good to miss!

LOOK FOR OUR FOUR FABULOUS MEN!

Each month some of today's bestselling authors bring
four new fabulous men to Harlequin American Romance.
Whether they're rebel ranchers, millionaire power brokers
or sexy single dads, they're all gallant princes—and
they're all ready to sweep you into lighthearted fantasies
and contemporary fairy tales where anything is possible
and where all your dreams come true!

You don't even have to make a wish…
Harlequin American Romance will grant your every desire!

Look for Harlequin American Romance
wherever Harlequin books are sold!

Harlequin Romance®

Delightful

Affectionate

Romantic

Emotional

Tender

Original

Daring

Riveting

Enchanting

Adventurous

Moving

Harlequin Romance—the
series that has it all!

HROM-G

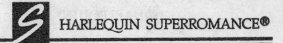

HARLEQUIN SUPERROMANCE®

...there's more to the story!

Superromance. A *big* satisfying read about unforget-
table characters. Each month we offer
four very different stories that range from family
drama to adventure and mystery, from highly emotional stories to romantic comedies—and
much more! Stories about people you'll
believe in and care about. Stories too
compelling to put down....

Our authors are among today's *best* romance writers. You'll find familiar names and
talented newcomers. Many of them are
award winners—and you'll see why!

If you want the biggest and best
in romance fiction, you'll get it
from Superromance!

Available wherever Harlequin books are sold.

◆ HARLEQUIN®

Not The Same Old Story!

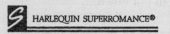 **HARLEQUIN ◆ PRESENTS®** Exciting, glamorous romance stories that take readers around the world.

◆ *Harlequin Romance*® Sparkling, fresh and tender love stories that bring you pure romance.

HARLEQUIN® *Temptation* Bold and adventurous—Temptation is strong women, bad boys, great sex!

S HARLEQUIN SUPERROMANCE® Provocative and realistic stories that celebrate life and love.

 **HARLEQUIN® AMERICAN ◆ ROMANCE®** Contemporary fairy tales—where anything is possible and where dreams come true.

 **HARLEQUIN® INTRIGUE®** Heart-stopping, suspenseful adventures that combine the best of romance and mystery.

 **LOVE & LAUGHTER™** Humorous and romantic stories that capture the lighter side of love.